SYMPHONY
OF
SHATTERING GLASS

For Giel, for sharing his stories.
For Sian, Maddie and my brothers for listening, reading, and supplying music.
For my parents for showing me how to love reading.
And especially for my wife for her inspiration and support; and my son, who roared at the hidden dragons.

SYMPHONY
OF
SHATTERING GLASS

Written and illustrated by

Gideon Kerk

SYMPHONY OF SHATTERING GLASS
Written and illustrated by
Gideon Kerk

A catalogue record for this book is available from The British Library

Published by Hope & Plum Publishing
www.hopeandplum.com

ISBN 978-1-9160363-6-9

'Don't hide your scars, because when you do, you're also hiding your stars. And they must shine. That's what stars are for. And scars. They make people who matter focus more on the shiny parts of you.' (page 51)

ONE

CRIMSON EVE

On Christmas Eve two dozen chickens and a duck were kidnapped. The kidnapper, however, considered it a temporary loan, rather than theft or abduction. In fact, she believed that the birds followed her willingly and the worms peeking out of her bulging pockets had nothing to do with it. The fact that it was the night before Christmas didn't make any difference to the thief either, as she had no idea what Christmas was.

'Ta-da. I introduce to you, *poultry-in-motion*,' the girl with the flaming hair said, her voice a song-web of excitement.

Think of a whirlwind pirouetting over red sand; or rather, think of a bonfire. Not a particularly large one, but not a small one either. To be precise, imagine it twelve-year-old-girl size, then you're about right. Give her rolled up flags for trousers and kindling for arms; one outstretched like a circus ringmaster introducing a daring act, then you picture the girl who confronted the boy at her bedroom door.

For a second, the boy just stood there, his hand still hovering next to his ear as if he was about to knock. Imprisoned by eyes deeper than the sea, he just about managed to blink, before the girl slammed the door shut, almost turning his nose into a knocker.

'Eulalie…' he hiccupped as an afterthought.

Eulalie wasn't a curse, or an exclamation, even though the peculiar word was frequently followed *by* an exclamation mark. It was, in fact, the girl's name and like most names, it fit her well. This one, however, was a bit more special than other names as it had already fit her before she had even been born.

Eulalie's momma had always said that it had been the gentle waves of the ocean lapping on the shore the night when she had turned from a mere, 'sparkle-in-my-eye' to a 'diamond-in-my-belly' that had whispered that name to her. When she had asked her momma what she meant, she had just smiled and said, 'Always remember that when people ask for your name, you should smile first; that'll make the wind blow. Then, after you've lent your name - you never *give* someone your name - remind them that they should say it like the wind and the waves would. It's a breathing-out whisper disguised as a word.'

Eulalie knew that there had been more to the story; the untold parts had always sparkled in her momma's eye like a tiny happy-ever-after diamond. Even though her momma had been gone for four years, twenty-one days and fourteen-and-a-half turns of the hourglass, those memories were clear as if they had only happened yesterday.

'Uhm...Eulalie?' the boy asked, his nose still inches from the wood. Two heartbeats later, the door swung open again.

'Ta-da!' Eulalie repeated, this time with even more heart and soul. Wind rattled her bedroom windows behind their locked shutters – there weren't any storms on the loose, so it must have been her smile that had made the winds change. 'I present to you...'

'*Poultry in motion?*' the boy finished her sentence but added the question mark.

'Well yes,' she said as if it was the most normal thing in the world to have a bedroom full of chickens. 'Don't just stand there and look at me like that. Come in, before one gets away.'

Violent curls of red hair bounced across Eulalie's eyes as she held the door and urged the boy to enter her room. A cloud of fluffy downs swirled around her as a chicken struggled under her armpit. Balancing on one foot that disappeared into a boot she could have bathed in, she was trying to herd two more chickens away from the door with the other bootless one. Toes afflicted with peculiar white freckles peeped through a hole in a frayed sock that resembled a dove's nest.

'Spookasem. Come in. Now,' she said.

Cluck.

It wasn't the boy who stood staring past her into the room who had answered. His mouth was hanging open, an assortment of words dangling from his lips. The fully-formed questions he would have asked lay at his feet. It was, of course, the chicken under the girl's arm who had made the comment.

The boy, Spookasem, had been the cause and excuse for countless moments of upheaval, but even he had never stared upon scenes of such havoc. In fact, if it wasn't for the shiver of excitement that surged through him at the sight of imminent disaster, he might even have been jealous.

'Eulalie.' Spookasem's lips finally found words in the kaleidoscope of confusion in his mind. 'I leave you for only a couple of hours and *this* is what you get up to?' He stretched his eyes wide and stole a step into the doorway; doorways were good places for asking questions. 'I *need* to be part of this. What can I do? Goats? Sheep? There's a donkey in a field not far from here. He'll be up for this; whatever *this* is. Some cows perhaps? Small ones. The big ones won't fit through the door.' Any adventure that began with a room full of chickens was bound to end in calamity; and if *he* wasn't the instigator, he most certainly wanted to share in the spoils, whether it ended in laughter, tears or a basket-full of bruises. Sharing it *all* was an Inkling's job after all.

Spookasem wasn't an ordinary boy. He was, in fact, an *Inkling* boy. Soon after Eulalie's momma had disappeared, her tutor, Mrs Sikkum, had given her a small bottle of blackest ink and a storm-cloud warning with a silver lining in her voice. 'Spilling anything is never pleasant,' Mrs Sikkum had said, in her customary sing-song tone. 'But spilling this shadow-ink could be perilous. Just a drop will do the trick.'

Eulalie, more curious than an unturned page, had of course spilt the ink on her bedsheets, and the Inkling boy had appeared, wearing disaster as a cape, just as Mrs Sikkum had warned. It had taken Eulalie six days to soak the stain out of the sheets before the boy had finally disappeared again. Two days later, after she had stitched up her frayed nerves, she dared summon the boy again. This time, however, she had taken care to feather only the tiniest drop onto the back of her hand. One lick and a quick rub on the back of her trousers could make him disappear before any potential disasters could fully form. Soon afterwards, every drop of ink turned from being a mere full stop, to everything from the rounding off of an epic adventure to the capital letter for the beginning of a new one.

Being more shadow and less boy, the clay-dough of Eulalie's imagination moulded Spookasem's blurry form into a mischievous thirteen-year-old. Soon, a pitch-perfect black fringe swayed heroically above almond eyes that could spot even unborn mischief. His smile was filled with already-formed retorts and ever-so-slightly pointy ears gave him the visage of the changeling prince from one of her fairy-tale books. And so, just like characters from fairy tales come-to-life in the minds and hearts of dreamers, Spookasem came to life for Eulalie. She was storm, he was cloud;

she was thunder, he was lightning, she was trouble, he was triple. Brewing together or bruising together, the two fit each other like pieces of a puzzle; a puzzle with as many pieces as there were stories and stars.

Cluck. Cluck. A high-pitched and drawn-out *cluuuck* made Eulalie release the struggling animal.

'Come on,' she said through gritted teeth and a cloud of downs. Grabbing Spookasem's arm she pulled him into her room.

TWO
A MASTEPLAN

'Merciful moonbeams. What in the name of...?' Spookasem asked, his head bobbing between the girl and the feathery pandemonium. 'Chickens? Why? What for? Where did you? *How* did you? And why have they been numbered?' he asked, struggling to grasp at the questions floating between all the feathers and clucks.

'Any news?' Eulalie asked, avoiding his questions.

She blew at the hair still hiding her face. The tangle of red parted, revealing a constellation of freckles and a peculiar white-stained skin-affliction. As if spilt by a clumsy artist, white lines, stains and splotches snowed over her eye and lashes, before being blown over faint scar lines that disappeared into a gap that used to be her ear.

Somewhere in her baby days – thankfully she couldn't remember any part of it - someone had attempted to rid her of this pale curse by burning her skin. The flames, however, didn't appear to have been much interested in the white stains, but had rather nibbled ravenously on her ear. At least her healthy ear was turned at a very good angle; anything worth listening to that might try to sneak past the missing ear was easily snapped up.

'So? Any news?' Eulalie repeated, failing to hide the hope in her voice. She busied her fingers with the buckles of her turtleneck capelet, but her eyes pleaded with the Inkling.

'This Scarlet Lockdown's got everyone spooked,' Spookasem said and dared a quick glance at Eulalie's unblinking eyes. He hated being the bearer of bad news. In this case, *no* news was *bad* news. He breathed in deep. 'Everyone's locked shop and bolted doors early. As always, the villagers are terrified of the monsters that the red moon is going to wake from hibernation.

9

Selkies, Howler Fey, Cinder Hounds…' his voice faltered. He knew that Eulalie was waiting for something else.

He sighed and Eulalie's shoulders slumped.

'And the noticeboards?' she asked in a voice frayed around the edges.

'Mostly the same as last Crimson Eve; just names of people lost in the red moonlight. I made sure your momma's still there. Went over it in dark ink. Someone had scribbled a note asking for anyone brave enough to go out into the red night to leave candles and gifts in the trees to lead the lost souls home,' Spookasem said. 'Even offering rewards for anyone found. No-one's willing to go out and search themselves though. Everyone's too scared.' Spookasem tugged the lock on the window. 'It's not only the monsters that frighten them, but you know how the moon-glow distorts time and warps the world; all those rumours about gates to other places opening and closing. The risks of getting lost are just too high.'

'No problem. We're brave enough,' Eulalie said. 'We don't need help; and we don't need any reward either.' She bit down on her disappointment with defiant lips and nudged a bag on the floor with her foot. 'Full of candles and presents. Now you know why I always volunteer to tidy the tavern in the mornings. I collect all the candle stumps. Most can still sing. Tonight we're gonna put far more candles in trees than ever.'

'And gifts?' Spookasem asked. He was trying his best to cheer her up.

'All done too. I've made some more walnut-glasses, mud-marbles, corn-dollies, a catapult, moss-mice and a book of fairy tales, just in case momma's out there.' Eulalie's face lit up in a sunrise memory, before that momentary joy once again set behind a horizon of brittle hope. 'I've wrapped all the gifts in leaves and spider-silk. Every present will be a surprise. I've written *For Momma* in large letters on a leaf-label on the book present,' Eulalie said. Speaking helped her hold onto her momma's warm memory-blanket.

Spookasem trapped her with his stare. 'I'm sorry that there wasn't any news, Freckles,' he said, putting an arm around her neck and sighed. A sigh could say far more than words. He filled this one with as much understanding as he could fit into a breath.

'Anyway, are you going to tell me about these chickens, or am I going to have to tickle the information out of you?' he asked, locking Eulalie in the crook of his arm with his threatening fingers wobbling in front of her face.

Eulalie wrestled herself free. There might not have been any news about her momma, but she was going to live as if there *was* good news. 'Not only chickens. There's also one duck...somewhere,' she said. As if on cue, a *quack* sounded a pitch or two above all the *clucks*.

A choppy sea of chickens swamped her room. Combs were swaying, wattles were bopping and spurs were fencing wherever Spookasem looked. They all also appeared to be pretty content with the strange labels that had been chalked onto their chest feathers.

P2 and *P7* had stamped themselves neighbouring nests in Eulalie's pillow and were snuggled deep in conversation, gossiping away in clucking quavers.

P5, *P6* and *P8* were dancing a jig on the torn bedside mat as if there were juicy worms hidden beneath – and there most probably were.

Both Eulalie and Spookasem had to jump out of the way as *P14* darted out from under the bed, pecking at a lacy petticoat that it had become tangled in. *P10* and *P17* gave chase pecking and squabbling as they attempted to steal the frilly flag from the fleeing *P14*, who was looking pretty well dressed for a chicken.

A duck's head appeared on its stem-of-a-neck growing to an impossible length out of an open bedside drawer.

'Is the duck also...?' Spookasem asked.

'Yes, Spook. The duck *is* also numbered - *H5*. I thought it would be a good idea to name them all. I started with the duck – called him *Hocus*. The chickens didn't want to stand still, so I got confused who was who. So, I decided to call them all *Pocus*.'

'*Hocus? Pocus?*' Spookasem asked. 'But that's not a name. It's a magic spell. You call everything *Hocus Pocus*. It's the name of that shipwreck-of-a-skiff of yours and I've heard you whisper *Hocus Pocus* to the moth that lives on the windowsill. Sometimes I can just shake my head in disbelief.' He shook his head in disbelief. He tutted too just to rub it in.

'It's not *really* a magic spell,' Eulalie said. 'It's more a word that wants to be a spell but is hiding a trick somewhere inside. Tonight, the chickens and the duck are gonna play a trick on everyone but us and almost like magic, they're gonna make us disappear. And anyway, my boat's *not* a shipwreck. I've rowed her before.'

'Yes, I *know*. And she sank. I was there, remember? On the bank, with dry feet. The only magic involved was the fact that I didn't laugh myself to death,' Spookasem said, his voice bursting with the joy of that memory.

12

'She didn't sink immediately.' Eulalie squinted at the Inkling, daring him to disagree.

'Anyway, *how's* the poultry gonna perform such a trick?' Spookasem asked.

'The numbers form the foundation of my master plan,' Eulalie said, drawing closer to the shadowy figure as if the walls had ears to listen in on her plan. 'Not long from now, my dadda's gonna turn the crimson hourglass and the church bells will chime.' She paused for dramatic effect. '*That*, as you know, means that Scarlet Lockdown has begun. Kahenna, the crimson moon will rise and I won't be allowed to leave the tavern until the moon has set again. Now, as he caught me *last* crimson moon on the roof and the one *before* that halfway up the chimney, he's gonna keep a close eye on me. He's already barred my window; every window. I've checked.' She folded her arms and eyed the window as if her stare could cut the lock.

'As I was saying,' Eulalie continued, 'my dadda and my *dearest* brother Lazaro will be keeping a close eye on me. The numbers on the chickens and the duck will be our distraction, because we've got to get out into the swamp tonight. We've got jobs to do. There are tracks to follow, candles to light, presents to deliver and people to rescue. *And* I need to leave the book for momma. I'll leave it close to the old mill. Maybe if she finds it there and sees the mill, she'll remember how to get home.'

Spookasem's face shone with bright adventure-excitement.

'So, once we're ready – and we've got to hurry – I'll set the chickens and the duck free, *inside* the tavern,' she said. 'My dadda wouldn't want the chickens pooping everywhere, so he'll be chasing them all night – and he'll be cursing Lazaro to help. The perfect distraction, it'll be easy to slip away. I've numbered them one to thirty-six.' She paused theatrically. 'I've left out the numbers thirteen, nineteen, no...maybe seventeen...or perhaps...oh I can't remember. Anyway, I've left out some numbers. The duck is number five. They'll be searching for the missing numbers and just like a magic trick, we'll be back before they've even caught half the chickens again.' Eulalie's face lit up.

'You're a genius,' Spookasem said. 'It's going to be our best adventure yet.'

Adventures were so much more fun when you shared them with your best friend, especially if your best friend ignored all the gaping holes in the plans too.

'But...but what about the birds? Won't your dadda...well...uhm...' Spookasem asked, pulling his finger across his throat while making a horrible squelching sound. 'They might end up as supper.'

'Nope. Thought of that too,' Eulalie said. 'The birds will be safe. Dadda's too superstitious. He'll never kill an animal on crimson night, just in case it's a cursed creature that's been woken by the moon. We'll chase them out once we're back and after the first rains, those numbers will be washed off too.' Her lips pulled into a stolen-milk smile.

'Good thinking, Freckles,' Spookasem said, sounding relieved. 'Let's pack.' The Inkling was hooked. It didn't take much to draw him into anything exciting – but sprinkle a little danger, stir in the possibility of a bruise or two and smear it with the promise of getting dirty and his blood boiled.

Distant church bells chimed, rooting the children on the spot. The chickens stopped, their crowns wobbled. They stretched their necks, their eyes searching for the terror that was about to unfold.

'The bells,' Eulalie said, her voice drowning in mystery.

'The countdown-drum's gonna start,' Spookasem said.

The bells stopped. Eulalie and Spookasem held their breaths.

THREE
SYMPHONY OF SHATTERING GLASS

The first *boom* made both children jump. Spookasem stifled a scream. The duck quacked off-key.

Boom! 'Eleven.' *Boom!* 'Ten.' *Boom!* 'Nine.' *Boom!* Eulalie and Spookasem breathed every number as if it were their last.

Every distant bellow-bark of the ancient warning drum cracked the unseen fabric of evening twilight as if breaking through ice. With the final, mournful beat, dusk shattered like a distant symphony of shattering glass. Eulalie flinched and clasped her heart while Spookasem ducked and flung his arms over his head. His misty body rippled and danced like smoke on a dying ember, before he formed into a boy again.

Kahenna, the crimson moon arrived, spilling the blood of the dying sunset over the horizon. The first crimson night creature raised its voice in a wakeful howl; a sleep-muffled wail welcoming Kahenna in a heart-wrenching lament.

'Eulaleee!' A sacrilege to the night, her dadda's voice took up where the creature's left off.

Eulalie swallowed the rest of the wonder away and her eyes grew wide. 'Dadda. That was dadda,' she said. She bit the side of a finger.

'And he only calls *three times*,' Spookasem echoed her dadda's motto.

'Quick Spook. We've still got lots to do and we're running out of time,' Eulalie warned, motivated into action; not by the mighty drumming of Kahenna's arrival, but by the threat of her dadda's footsteps that would soon be drumming down the corridor.

*

A little moth outside Eulalie's window stirred. Lifting a fluffy, sleepy head, it ruffled its fern-like antennae with tiny gloved hands. The red light of Kahenna's stare blanketed the tiny creature in a rippling ruby glow. Its shadow grew and stretched onto the chimney wall next to the window ledge. The shadow shrugged off a moth-like hood revealing what might have been a little person with wings. It appeared to yawn and stretch, before leaning towards the window to peep through the gap in the locked shutters.

*

Chop. Chop. Chop. Eulalie's heart beat in time with Spookasem's slicing of carrots and parsnips into vegetable-coins.

Chop. Chop. The Inkling stopped and looked down. Eulalie was half under her bed, reaching for something. 'I still don't know why these carrot-and-parsnip coins are necessary. We've never seen the Gatekeeper. Don't even know if he exists,' Spookasem said and popped a coin into his mouth.

Eulalie turned a face, deeply shaded in beetroot, towards the Inkling. 'My green fairy-tale book says there's one. He's just busy *and* things change on a crimson night. The gate keeps moving, otherwise people wouldn't get stuck there, now would they?' she said, brandishing a sash laden with pouches and buckles.

Spookasem opened his mouth to argue, but thought better of it and flicked a parsnip coin into his mouth instead. The rest he swept into a little pouch and lobbed it at Eulalie. She put it in one of the pockets of her sash. The others bulged with glass bottles that the leather flaps struggled to conceal.

'Fairy-flasks for *magic dust*, nixie-jars for *sands of time* and pixie-pots for *fragments of moonlight;* just in case we come across any of them in the enchanted night,' Eulalie explained, tapping each pouch just to make sure they were secure. 'The moth that lives on the sill loved the *fragments of moonlight* that I collected from a moon puddle the last time we managed to sneak out.'

'And crocodile tears?' Spookasem asked.

'Well, if we stumble across a crying crocodile, we could try and get a few drops,' she replied.

Spookasem coughed to stifle his gulp. 'I'm gonna stay behind for a while,' he said. 'To keep an eye on the poultry; make sure they're safe performing their not-so-magic trick. Where should I meet you?'

Eulalie took a piece of paper out of her pocket and unfolded it on the floor. The Inkling recognised the strange map immediately; *London Underground Mind the Gap Map.* It was on one of their earlier Scarlet Lockdown adventures that they had stumbled upon the peculiar map lying in a muddy monster footprint. After careful contemplation, they had settled on the notion that it was a map of their swampland. With a bit of squinting and a lot of imagination, gnarled trees, farm fences, clearings and derelict farm-houses turned into Royal Oak, Sloane Square, Parson's Green and Swiss Cottage.

Eulalie's finger imprisoned a point on the map. 'I'm going to the derelict mill first. To drop off the book and to pick something up.'

Spookasem inhaled a question, but a creaking floorboard deflated his curiosity.

'Then I'm following Queens Way. All along this red line. Marble Arch, Lancaster Gate, Notting Hill Gate and finally

Shepherd's Bush,' she said, her stained finger tapping her route on the map. 'I'll put candles in the trees along the way. Follow the candles or follow the string. I'll uncoil it so it's impossible for us to get lost.'

She folded the map and slipped it into her pocket. 'Got it?' she asked.

'Got it,' Spookasem answered.

'Eulalie, you know I only call three times!' Eulalie's dadda's dark bellow reverberated through the hallway and bullied its way into her room.

Spookasem stumbled and Eulalie's heart skipped a beat. She actually grabbed at her chest, just in case her heart crashed through.

'Where's my hat? My hat?' Eulalie's voice was peppered in rising panic.

'In your hand,' Spookasem said.

A theatrical swing later, the floppy red cap was on her head, angled over one side of her face, the shadows hiding her identity, but shading her in glory.

'Ready,' she said in a low growl.

The strained voices of the floorboards in the hallway called their warning. Distant at first, each new voice sounding more terrified than the one before.

'Your boot. You're still only wearing one Swamp-Trotter. Your toes are still showing.' Spookasem clutched his head in exasperation.

The last buffalo poop Eulalie had stepped in helped them track the boot down in no time.

Tap, crunch, squeek.

'He's close,' Eulalie whispered.

'Who?' the Inkling asked. He had forgotten to breathe.

'Lazaro.' Eulalie said her brother's name like the first-sting-of-a-nettle.

Eyeing the door, Eulalie knelt down, picked up her small bow and poop-tipped arrows and slipped them into her bag of gifts. Being blunt and padded in buffalo poop, the arrows might have appeared harmless. Their secret, however, wasn't sticking to the target, but *stinking* the target.

Tap, crunch, squeek.

Eulalie crept closer to the door, dragging behind her an Inkling and a mantle of poultry.

She pushed her healthy ear to the wood.

Tap. Crunch. Squeek.

'Lazaro's trying to sneak up on you,' Spookasem whispered. 'Sneaking is a skill. He must have other talents.'

'Yip. He's getting ready for Dadda's final call. Making sure I don't get away.'

Unknown to them, Lazaro was eavesdropping on the other side of the door; his ear mere inches away.

'Eulalie. Who're you talking to? Who's in there with you?' Lazaro asked through the wood. He tried to sound brave, but his words shivered, spilling crumbs of courage. 'Dadda, Dadda, Eulalie's got someone in her room. Or she's talking to herself again. It's the lunar lunacy. We should summon the priest,' he called.

'Remember to check my drop of ink *all-the-time*,' Spookasem whispered. 'If it washes off, I'll disappear and I don't want to miss a thing.'

Eulalie looked at the freckle of dry ink on her palm, tapped her pocket to feel for the bottle of ink. Still there. She nodded. She pursed her lips. Her duffle bag was full of gifts and it rested comfortably over her shoulder and chest. Her mind bulged with plans and her heart drummed the rhythm of adventure.

'Daddaaa! Eulalie's up to someth...'

Eulalie didn't allow Lazaro to finish his sentence. In one, swift and practiced movement, she flicked the latch and ripped the door open.

The brief glimpse into Eulalie's room allowed a moment for Lazaro's eyes to fall on Eulalie *and* a strange shadow that appeared to belong to no-one; a shadow that didn't stretch out, flatten and elongate on the floor, but appeared to be standing *upright* next to his sister. Spookasem, was of course supposed to be invisible to everyone apart from Eulalie, but strange things happened on crimson nights.

'B ...B... Boggaaaart! Eulalie's let a boggart into the tavern. Grab your sword. Evacuate,' Lazaro screamed and stumbled into the hallway wall.

'Boggart?' Spookasem asked and folded his arms. 'I don't look anything like a boggart.' He smoothed his fringe as if to make sure.

Moments later, the chickens charged. Lazaro's scream – a beautiful, crystal clear note graced the second floor of their tavern, *The Cross in the Roads*. Then he was wrapped in a dough of shadows, sautéed in downs, simmered in *clucks*, skewered on chicken claws and topped with a dollop of bird-poo sauce.

*

The full force of Kahenna's dangerous light slammed into Eulalie the moment she whisper-footed out of the kitchen door. Alien sounds knit in and out of blankets of hovering mist while strange howls and hoots weaved a cotton dream-web between the trees. Pointed twig-fingers beckoned her to come closer while gnarled branches held aloft palms of warning to stay put.

For just a heartbeat she hesitated at the bottom of the steps. Behind her was confined chaos and *definitely* bruises in the tavern and in front of her, vast uncertainty and *most probably* bruises. But adventure too.

Decision made, she inhaled deeply, filling her lungs with the crimson perfume of dry ash and flameless sparks. Then, she sidestepped the enormous wooden beams that held the tavern above the tidewaters and ducked her head under *The Cross in the Roads*.

Embraced by the tavern's shadows, Eulalie closed her eyes for a moment to admire the chorus of chaos above. The orchestra of thumps made the tavern sound as if it was rolling down a hill. Maybe it was her imagination, but she was certain that she heard clucks and quacks stirred into the soup of mayhem. Little did everyone know that the poet of the palaver was just inches beneath their feet.

Eulalie's Swamp-Trotters were so full of holes that her feet were already wet through. She didn't mind though. Quests that started with wet feet could only get better.

Then Eulalie's eyes settled on the second part of her

escape plan.

'My sweet *Hocus Pocus*,' she filled her voice with a barrel of joy and kneeled down next to her beloved skiff. She stroked the old wood. Barely recognisable as a rowing boat, this wounded mass of planks was miraculously held together by far stronger stuff than its brass corsets and rusty nails. Her planks held fast and keel cut true by the force of the wild imagination and unfathomable faith of the flaming-haired child who cared so much for her. Her boat was full of potential and *that* was a perfect place for dreams to start. Eulalie dreamed of restoring her to her former glory – whatever that might have been – but at present, *Hocus Pocus* only stayed afloat for a few heartbeats before becoming barnacle-bait.

Even if she *had* been able to glide on water, Eulalie had different plans for her this Crimson Eve. Yes, *Hocus Pocus* had a secret that not even Spookasem knew about. The Inkling might doubt the boat's ability to swim again one day, but he couldn't criticize the boat's ability to disguise itself as a mighty dragon.

FOUR

THE MIGHTY DRAGON

Tap. Tap. Tap. Tap. Tap. Tap. Tap.

Eulalie glanced up at the underside of the tavern and smiled. She was in a secret place beneath the tavern. The ancient building moaned as it slowly rocked from side to side on its stilt-legs as if trying to oil its rusty joints. Craning her neck, she listened to the footsteps inside the tavern drumming on the floor-boards above her. Footsteps were see-through; they betrayed a lot about their owner. Lazaro's sounded like the end of a song, the last beats, the running-away part. Brave footprints sounded like the beginning of a song; full of potential with a running-towards-tempo. Giggling into her cupped hand and squealing with excitement, she realised that Lazaro was right above her – right at the window at the bar counter where her telescope stood guard. 'Don't you dare touch my telescope,' she said. As if she could see through the patched and gnarled wood, she squinted her eyes at the belly of the tavern

Fuming as though she had already found his prints on its pristine brass body, she gripped the starboard gunwale of *Hocus Pocus* and pushed.

The boat resisted for only a moment, before allowing Eulalie to tip her over. With a dull thud she landed upside down, revealing her secret side. With the ancient wood half-rotten and soft, Eulalie had managed to shape the rudder into the head of a snarling dragon and carve the keel into its humps. In the dim light, tricked by shadows and outlined by the cleverness of silhouettes, she marveled at her sculpture.

In a flash she had a thin blue chord attached to one of the tavern's stilts; she would uncoil the ball of string as she went along. Just in case the Gatekeeper didn't like vegetables, she'd be able to lead them home by following the line.

Wet knees, scraped palms and a bump to the head later, she was under the boat, peeping through one of the holes in the hull – one that she was now glad she hadn't patched yet.

Eulalie took one, two, three deep breaths and with a grunt, she crawled forwards, her head pushing on the inside of the boat. Draped and cloaked in *Hocus Pocus*, Eulalie inched her way from under the tavern.

Her breathing sounded like a storm in a jar in the wooden confinement. Her imagination ran wild imagining her skiff resembled a terrifying beast crawling out from her shadowy cocoon.

Kahenna, the crimson moon loved games, especially those that involved monsters, and decided to play along. She opened her crimson eye wide, casting a stretched spotlight of red in the wake of the boat-beast. She sickle-smiled; the image looked marvelous. Her light burned in flames of ruby where they reflected off the water-filled puddle-prints left by Eulalie's large boots. The drag-line left in the wet mud by the stern of the boat lit up as if the monster was robed in a bleeding cloak. If only Eulalie had been a fly on the wall, she would have been awed at how close her wish of that moment had been to reality.

'Find your sister,' she heard her dadda's voice in the distance. Anyone else would have thought that it was merely a distant bark. Eulalie knew better. Barks belonged to dogs. Dogs were loyal and cuddly.

'Oh no, oh no, oh no,' she said and crawled faster.

'I don't care if Kahenna pukes a barrel of red on you. Open that cursed window and see if she's out there,' her dadda shouted. His voice sounded as if he was about to burst.

A window shutter slammed open. Eulalie jumped and bumped her nose into the wood. For a moment she thought that perhaps her dadda *had* burst, but then she heard the scream. It was one of those screams that somehow lingered like unseen footprints in the air; she wasn't quite sure when it ended and its echo started.

Eulalie smiled and inched her way towards her mill.

Determined and excited, the scraping of her upside-down boat drowned out the alien sounds of crimson night. Bestial calls echoed in and out of mist-ghosts that hovered over streams and puddles. Leathery wings fluttered in drunken whisper-paths overhead, dodging stretched branch-arms and spider-webs. Secret whispers continued the haunting tales they had begun the last time Kahenna was visiting. Creatures were still waking, flexing arms, claws, legs or wings and their yawns joined the crimson orchestra. Those who had already shaken the dream-dust from their eyes, hop-scotched and pitter-pattered in tiny footsteps dancing in parade along the sparkling trail left in the wake of this strange new creature – a creature that looked like a dragon, sounded like wood, but smelled like a child, perfumed with adventure.

*

*P7 w*as without a shadow of a doubt the fastest chicken. She moved with expert ease, swerving before the brain could even fathom whether she was feigning left and turning right or feigning right and turning left. Spookasem marveled at her moves; he made a mental note to try them later himself.

About to make his own getaway, the Inkling cast a nervous glance at the large, ancient hourglass that was counting away the nightmarish hours of Scarlet Lockdown with its bleeding sands. He still had lots of time – the night was still young – a spring chicken. He giggled at his own joke. Within the light of the Crimson Moon, he knew that time did funny things anyway. All he needed to do was step into Kahenna's light before the moon set, and he would be fine – one could spend what felt like days there in a mere night.

He decided to linger a bit longer to be able to witness such a poetic – or rather *poultry-etic* - spectacle in the tavern. He chuckled at his own joke again and wished that Eulalie was there to share in his cleverness.

The out-of-tune solo of curses belched out by Eulalie's dadda, Esau, was accompanied by Lazaro's attempt at backing vocals. In a corner shivering in candle-light, two musicians felt inspired by the pandemonium and snatched up their instruments. The fiddler winked at the accordionist and moments later a marginally more musical wail joined the melting pot of commotion. Spookasem winced as he suddenly flickered like a flame chewing on the dregs of a wick. 'Blessed moons. My ink. My ink's washing off.' He slid off the counter and headed for the door.

'Eulalie!' Esau bellowed, 'This unholy mischief has her stamp all over it. Lazaro. Find that pathetic excuse of a sister. She's gone too far this time. I'll…' No one heard what he would do, though, because his grumbles were lost in a cacophony of breaking glass as the flustered hen Esau was swatting at knocked over a carefully stacked pyramid of glasses.

'She's not here. I've looked everywhere… she's not in any of the attics either. I think she got out,' Lazaro whined.

A large man at the bar shivered and took a reassuring drink from his tankard and then rested it on his belly. 'Wherever that girl is, she wouldn't be stupid enough to be out in the crimson. Will be somewhere in the tavern colluding with the chickens...'

'Well if she's out there, we won't be seeing her again. She'd be just a pile of bones by sunrise. Good riddance I say.'

'Diseased child …'

'Moon-plagued … quite mad …'

'Unholy stains …'

Spookasem didn't want to hear any more. He flickered again. He needed to get to Eulalie. The patrons looked towards the door; they had either heard the click of the latch as he slipped out or the drumbeat of his heart.

FIVE
THE JESTER, THE PUPPETEER AND THE MARIONETTE

Click. Click. Clack.

The child sat up. For two heartbeats he didn't know where he was. 'Must've been dreaming,' he said to the starlight. His lips smacked together as he chewed on the hunger in his empty mouth.

Even though famished, he was still too exhausted to get up. Pulling his quilt - roughly woven together out of moss and crimson moonbeams - to his chin, he was about to surrender to sleep rather than hunger when …

Click. Click. Clack.

That last *clack* got his attention. It echoed with promise, potential. It appeared to emanate from a little spark of lightning. He urged his eyes through his nest of mistletoe that was snuggled high up in the arms of a fir tree. Kahenna's stare had painted the leafy walls red. He liked it.

Click! Click! Clack!

Yes. There it was again. Sleep…hunger…curiosity. Curiosity won.

Without a sound, he hopped out of his cosy nest and stepped onto the breeze. He inhaled a great gulp of Kahenna's candyfloss sweet air, took hold of a bunch of shadows and danced with the crimson moonlight towards the strange sound.

'Wynter, where are you going?' a gossamer voice asked. 'Hurry back. We'll have to go and search for food soon.

*

Click! Click! Clack!

'Finally. Hello little one,' Eulalie said to the new-born flame and dropped her flint and steel. The ember blinked and yawned itself into a little flame that shivered in new wakefulness.

'Merry Crimson Eve, little friend,' she said. The flame blinked sleepy eyes, coughing sparks and spilling shadows all over the walls of the derelict mill. Eulalie lifted her lantern and placed the candle inside. To prevent too much light from giving her away, she had veiled the glass with young leaves. She placed it on the low wall. Then she moved aside a curtain of ivy, to reveal a gap in the stonework. Her eager hands reached inside the wall and lifted out a melon-sized bundle. Wrapped-and-strapped in cloth, chord and secrets, it was bursting with promise.

Within moments, she had it unwrapped, revealing a tidy pile of coloured glass rectangles, each about the size of her palm. The candle light peeked through its leafy eye-patch in curiosity, reflecting off Eulalie's most valuable possession as if she had just unwrapped a fallen star.

'Tonight, I'll take this one, this one and… maybe… this one,' Eulalie said to herself, picking three glass rectangles that were to accompany her on the night's adventure. She put them aside. Then, not wanting the others to feel left out, she snuggled the bunch to her cheek. 'I'm sorry I can't take all of you. Your time will come.' The glass clinked together in understanding.

Eulalie and her momma had discovered the glass shapes in a hidden attic of the ancient mill with a bunch of old, hand-made children's toys. The toys were interesting, but the beautiful glass rectangles set off all sorts of storms in her mind and music in her heart.

Each piece of glass was inscribed with intriguing smoke-like writing that danced frames around mysterious pictures. Half-moon dolphins, large birds, musical instruments, skies full of stars, uncertain moons and confident suns were but few of the images that graced each shiny surface. They were dreams and nightmares at the same time; each pane telling its tale in a chaotic ocean of colours, as dots and lines seemed to sing their way between these strange glass worlds.

After their discovery, Eulalie and her momma had spent many days trying to figure out the nature of their true identity. At first, they thought they were pieces of a puzzle; then they turned into the crystal pages of an enchanted book; soon they had become dreams that had dripped from the stars and frozen over. It was wonderful to climb the stairs of their imaginations and explore fantasies that were hidden behind dusty dream-doors.

Once a fortune-teller with a dreamy voice and a pack of cards filled with promises had visited the tavern. That was when Eulalie had decided that her glass shards must be playing cards; very special ones too. Just the right size and full of potential, the pictures, patterns and satisfying feel of the peculiar glass objects had opened new windows in her imagination. Soon after, she and her momma had invented card games with them, making rules as they went along; as those were the most fun games anyway. Most importantly, though, the glass now reflected the memory of those days spent with her momma, as if her love had embedded itself within the glass.

As if storing delicate memories, Eulalie wrapped them again and placed the precious bundle back inside the wall. Once back in place, she ruffled the ivy veil so that the wall looked undisturbed.

Her eyes then found the three glass shards she had kept out. There was something about these that always made her feel cotton wool safe, dispelling ink-dark thoughts and weaving colour into her courage.

One by one she lifted each to the lantern light. On the first, a young puppeteer with a many-pointed hat and a donkey-puppet-for-a-hand was sitting curled up, knees under his chin. A mouse was watching his puppet-show from his curly shoe.

The second depicted the same puppeteer walking on stilts, while blowing a dandelion clock. A marionette danced in the dandelion-snow.

On the third card, the boy was dressed as a court jester and was balancing on a tightrope that was slung between two stars. A smiling moon was watching his daring act.

Eulalie's favourite of the three was the puppeteer and his mouse. A tender smile failed to hide her feelings for the strange boy on the glass. She admired it one more time. Unknown to her, the lantern light cast a projection of the picture through the little stained glass onto her face. There the mouse bounced off the puppeteer's shoe, happily received a morsel of food from him, before hopping from freckle to freckle back to the pointy shoe.

Eulalie glanced around shyly and planted a quick kiss onto the picture of the puppeteer. Her cheeks ignited and her heart played a jack-rabbit rhythm.

Moments later, Eulalie had some twine woven through tiny holes that peeked through each of the four corners and she hung them around her neck. She wasn't afraid of the cards breaking. Once she had accidentally dropped the whole stack from a tall tree and not a single one had even chipped.

Next, Eulalie dragged *Hocus Pocus* into the room; she had to angle her through the door. It was Crimson Night after all, and she didn't want anyone... or rather *anything* stealing her boat – or worse. Though, it would be quite exciting if some monstrous creature decided to hibernate in her boat.

'Nearly there,' she said to *Hocus Pocus*, shifting aside a rotting mat with her boot to reveal a trapdoor in the floor. The thick wood was darkened by age and wrinkled with the burden of the secrets that it hid beneath the mill. Its rusty hinged bones creaked as she lifted it up and rested it against the mossy wall. Below lay a stony decline that led towards a watery tunnel and a shimmering shroud of darkness.

Eulalie's boat appeared reluctant to slide into the dark. 'Come on,' she encouraged. 'You've never complained before.' She pushed, her boots slipping, until the boat finally relented and slid down the slope, pulling Eulalie with her. It was fun, even though she nearly lost a boot.

In a moss-muffled splash, the boat came to a halt in shallow water. Eulalie held her back before she decided to try and swim deeper into the tunnel. The water rippled like a legion of knights in armour on the march under a starless sky.

Eulalie tied *Hocus Pocus* to the mill's gigantic water wheel that lived in that dripping underground world. This enormous scoop wheel loomed to one side, its top disappearing into the arched ceiling, its lower end permanently hidden beneath the water.

In days long forgotten, when the mill wasn't merely the inspiration for ghost stories, it's sails would have turned majestically in the wind, setting in motion hinges, cogs, springs and wheels, all hidden somewhere in its large body. Her momma had explained to her that the mill's intricate design was specially made to turn the scoop wheel. This wheel would collect the water and send it on its journey into the canal and back out to sea to help keep the village, Huddle, fairly dry.

On windy days when the sails rocked and swayed, Eulalie would swear that she could hear some of those cogs itching to stretch their bones and turn again. In spite of imagining how majestic the mill would have looked it its day and longing to see the mechanism work, Eulalie suspected that if the sails were to turn and set the wheel in motion, it would most probably bring the whole mill down.

Eulalie glanced along the glinting channel that led under the mill and caught sight of Kahenna's red glow through the barred opening at the distant end of the arched tunnel where it met the canal.

'Now don't go sailing off on any of your own adventures,' she told her dragon. 'You know you'd only sink again.' With a final see-you-later tap on the boat's wooden shoulder, she skipped back up the incline, stopping next to the scoop wheel. There her eyes darted to the writing on the opposite wall. The scraped warning was worn and smoothed by the hands of time, but with the help of shadows still clear enough to read. Eulalie loved how the tails of the *t's, s's and 'h's* coiled as if written in flame and smoke.

'*Beware the wind that blows from where the red moon rises.*' Eulalie whispered those words as if they were holy, a prayer to set her up for her night's adventures. Then she hopped up the ramp and dropped the trapdoor shut.

Once the tatty mat was back in place again, she barred the door from the inside; it was the only door that led into this room of hers. A heartbeat later, the room lay empty and undisturbed; the only movement coming from a boot disappearing through a hole in the roof.

39

SIX
OLD KNEE-CAP

'Your arms look tired tonight,' Eulalie said to the gnarled tree that she called *Old Knee-Cap*. She shook his twiggy hand; kindness was like a wheel, sooner or later it rolled back to you. The bog-pine looked almost exactly like a tired old man sitting in shallow water, trunk bent with age. 'Don't worry. I won't burden you with anything heavy to carry,' she spoke to her rooty old friend. 'Just a candle to shine a halo of hope. Remember to point the way towards *The Cross in the Roads* if anyone comes past.'

In a flash, she lit a candle, dripped some wax onto one of his knee-roots and pushed the candle into it. Eulalie selected the book-shaped gift from the hessian duffle bag. 'And this is for momma. But anyone can read it if they want to.' She rested it in *Old Knee-Cap's* twiggy hands. 'May this remind you to come home,' Eulalie said. She pinched her eyes shut as she sent her dream to drift with the mist. Her knuckles turned white as she clutched the glass rectangles to her heart, blessing her wishes with as much hope as she could muster.

Satisfied, she hugged the old tree and gave him a peck on the cheek.

With a theatrical flourish, she flung her bag over one shoulder; and over the other, a long stick holding the twine that was still attached to the post at the tavern. The lantern now dangled on the end of the stick too. Once her eyes became accustomed to Kahenna's stare, she didn't need a lantern to see by – it served another *defensive* purpose. She calculated that the light behind her would send a long shadow out in front of her, thereby chasing anything away before she got there. At the same time, anything or anyone coming up behind her might think she were holding the lamp out in front of her and walking backwards.

Therefore, she wouldn't be sprung upon from the front, nor snuck up on from behind.

With a whistle in her heart, a hop in her tread and a frayed blue line keeping her attached to the real world, she set off along the feint path deeper into Kahenna's dream-world.

Little did she know that the lantern-plan had the *opposite* effect. A chorus of little creatures fluttered in the halo of light within moments, enjoying the playful swing of the lantern and its warming laughter. Some had large eyes and little wings, others pointy ears and large wings, and a few had dangling arms and spindly legs. Further along the path, her outstretched shadow was secretly holding hands with a fat, fluffy creature that was ambling along with them on the left side and a hunched-over scaly beast with a long thin tongue on the right.

*

The twin aspen trees, *Quiver* and *Barky*, always looked magical as they leaned against each other, two large branches crossing like children with arms slung over each other's shoulders.

This was *Marble Arch* and this was always the place where Eulalie had imagined the Gatekeeper would be waiting. She was a little disappointed that he wasn't there but she left a handful of vegetable coins in a hole in the trunk anyway. 'Toll paid,' she said to the arch.

Eulalie was about to clamber up the tree towards the bow where she was planning to leave some candles, when something ruffled *Barky's* leafy fringe. She held her breath. *Was it the Gatekeeper?*

'G…good evening.' She wasn't sure how to address the

Gatekeeper. She took a breath and tried to weave a bit more confidence into her voice. 'I…I wasn't sure whether I should pay you now, or once I need to get back home again – so I've left some coins for you here in the tree.' Eulalie pointed.

'Blindfold, blindfold, guide me through the bells,

Acorns, round stones, pretty sea-shells,' a child sang.

Eulalie knew that rhyme. It was from a game kids played in the woods blindfolded. They scrambled through the undergrowth to be the first to find an acorn, a round stone and a shell without touching a bluebell. The child who won the previous round got to remove their blindfold and take a turn acting as the judge. The game, however, often ended up with fists flying, tears spilling and barrels-full of cheating.

Without making it appear too obvious, Eulalie shifted in an attempt to identify the singer.

'Cut the string, flap the wing, don't step into a fairy ring,' Eulalie whispered, continuing the rhyme.

'Mermenin scales, hard as nails, shares the name with garden snails,' the child sang again, high pitched excitement nudging his voice off key.

Eulalie ducked as an explosion of leaves rained down on her. Bare feet slipped through *Barky*'s beard and moments later a child landed in front of her.

SEVEN

GIFTS, CANDLES AND TREES

For a breath each stared at the other in stunned silence. Eulalie's momma taught her that good introductions were always important – first impressions set the tone for the rest of the interaction. So she stuck out her hand to greet the little boy. 'Hello. My name's Eulalie.'

He frowned and looked at her hand with feline curiosity. Even though quite a bit younger, the strange boy had an antiquity in his face that seemed to leak from the ancient depths of his eyes; eyes that drowned in an eternity of blue.

'No. That's not how you play the game,' he said, 'I've found one of the three. You must guess first which it is. I will give it to you once you've guessed. That is, if your guess is right.... correct I mean, because it could be in the left.' He held out both hands balled into fists. There didn't appear to be enough space on his face to contain all the mischief and secrets he was trying to hide; some escaped through a cheeky grin.

'Uhm…sorry…' Eulalie dropped her hand. Her cheeks warmed up. 'I was just introduc…'

'Wynter. I'm Wynter. You woke me when you called the flame in your lantern with your lightning kisses. Now guess,' he said.

Eulalie watched his eyes flicking to his left hand. Was it a trick, or had she caught him out? Now, drawn into the game, Eulalie actually felt a bit nervous.

'I…I think it's …a… shell. It's a sea shell and it's in *this* hand. She reached for the left, but at the last moment, he shuffled over and she touched his right hand. Eulalie said, 'hey, that's cheating…'

'Good guess,' Wynter said. He opened up his right hand

and a shiny shell lay in his dirty palm. 'Very good guess. How'd you know?'

'I … don't … kn….' Eulalie's words stumbled.

'Never mind. Here. It's yours,' Wynter said.

Eulalie couldn't pull away. In a heartbeat, he had grabbed her hand and shoved the shell inside. The skin of his palm felt rough – he must love climbing trees. She saw that there was also a shell in his left hand.

'Thank you…' Eulalie said, wondering whether she should give him a gift too. 'Are you … the Gatekeeper?'

He gave her a stolen-chocolate smile. 'No, silly. He has blue hair; shiny. He's most probably fishing. You know, he eats the fish *raw*,' he said, sounding not too pleased about the Gatekeeper's apparent choice of food.

Eulalie's eyes bulged. Was it true or was the boy teasing her? 'How old are you?' she asked him and squinted, trying to find any lie-lines on his face.

'Seven,' he said and held up his open hand, showing five fingers.

Eulalie put her hands on her hips and a sliver of lantern-light danced up her cheek.

'Your face,' Wynter gasped. He moved his head to peek past the shadows and touched his eye-lid and forehead, exactly where Eulalie's white stains and scars were. 'Your face is….'

'Stained. I know.' Eulalie salted her voice. He was most probably just like her brother and was trying to think of some silly insult.

'Beautiful,' he continued, ignoring Eulalie's rising fury. 'We don't look up enough. Most of our lives we look down – where we're walking, what's growing, who's hiding, avoiding poop - so sometimes the stars need to remind us that we come from up there.' He pointed at the stars. 'So, the stars remind us through people like you.'

Eulalie was stunned. In fact, she had to shake her head as the impact of the words had made the world feel unsteady.

'You shouldn't cover your face in shadows,' he said. 'You're making the shadows feel guilty for hiding you. They don't want to.'

Eulalie touched the tip of her cap and moved the hat up, revealing more of her stained face.   'Anyway, what are you doing? I can help,' Wynter said, picking up the candles she had dropped when he had shoved the shell into her hand.

'I'm...I want to put candles all along the arch of the touching branches...'she said, still stumbling over the compliment he had given her.

Wynter's eyes lit up. 'Let me help. A crown of candles.' Moments later he was sitting where *Quiver* and *Barky* touched, busying himself squeezing candles between the dents and folds of the old wood.

Wynter's writhing around in the branches and leaves had cleared a leafy path for a brilliant ruby ray of moonlight to stretch through the tree's canopy and leak onto the swamp floor. Where the gossamer fingers of crimson light caressed the ground, a peculiar puddle formed.

'Strings of life dripping into a moon-puddle,' Eulalie whispered as her fingers automatically fumbled with a buckle on one of the pouches to free some of her vials. Her gaze followed sparkles of dust dancing between the wisps of mist. Together they waltzed down the moon-path until they disappeared into the magical water world that the moon had unlocked at her feet.

Eulalie finally managed to free a pot and a bottle. She uncorked the pot, held it an angle and allowed some light to kiss the pot's lip. A heartbeat later, she stoppered it. Then, kneeling down, she flicked open the bottle and dipped it into the moon water. It drank greedily. Filled to the brim, she smoothed its lip and licked the red water off her finger, before closing it again Safely stashing the pot and the bottle, she stood up. It wasn't a moment too soon. 'Finished. Wow, look at our masterpiece,' Wynter said.

Eulalie looked up. Wynter stretched his arms out wide, embracing the brilliant joy of light blazing from the tiara of candles on the crossing branch-frame. The leaves behind him shifted back into position, cutting off the moonlight and moments later, the little moon-puddle dried up.

'Thank you, Wynter,' Eulalie said. She wasn't only thanking the strange boy for his help with the candles, but also for what he had said to her earlier – she was a bit cautious to verbalise it exactly, just in case he hadn't actually meant it as a compliment. Eulalie was used to bruises caused by nasty words, insults and evil jokes, but wasn't quite sure how to nurture compliments. This one felt like a mouthful of balled sugar and her head was spinning with its unaccustomed sweetness.

Wynter dropped to the ground and turned to Eulalie. A hundred questions pulled into his face. 'Who is the present for?' he asked. They both looked up. Right beneath them hung one of the presents that Eulalie had wrapped in cobwebs.

'It's... well... for anyone,' she answered.

'Even me? So, I can just… take it?' Even though the boy sounded very keen, he didn't reach for it, but eyed Eulalie side-on. Was he testing her?'

'Uhm… yes. Of course, you can take it,' Eulalie said. 'But, only if you're lost. Are you lost?' This might be Eulalie's chance to lead someone home.

The boy thought for a moment and then said, 'No, I'm not lost. My home's up there.' He pointed up with a dirty finger. 'But if I find someone who *is* lost, I'll guide them to the candles and the present.' That idea lit him up. 'We all will.'

Eulalie followed his gaze to a nearby tree. It was pretty dark, but she was almost certain she saw a small round face peeking at them through a dense bush of mistletoe. Eulalie made out a pair of turquoise eyes, but they vanished amid a rustle of giggles.

'Thank you. That'll be very helpful, indeed,' she said, regarding Wynter again. She believed him. Somehow, he didn't appear to be lost. She had never seen anyone who looked like him before. She couldn't put her finger on it, but he just looked like someone at home in Kahenna's light.

A strange growling sound made Eulalie jump. 'What was th…' She swallowed those last words. Even in the dim light, she saw Wynter's face darken as the curse of embarrassment flooded him. He rubbed his stomach and smiled.

'My stomach seems to be complaining,' he said. 'Empty like a cloudless night it has space for a storm; sounds like one too.'

'Wait a moment,' Eulalie said. Her hand dived into her bag and moments later she offered him the remaining vegetable coins.

'For me? Are you giving *me* a present?' Wynter's voice

betrayed the fact that he wasn't used to receiving gifts.

'Yes. This is for you. It was meant to be for the Gatekeeper, but I feel that you might need it more than him,' Eulalie said. 'Sorry it's not much.'

Wynter reached for the gifts but clasped her hands in his. Their eyes met. He held her gaze for a moment, sneaked a peek at the glass rectangles around her neck and before she could look away, he cradled her gaze again.

Eulalie saw his ancient eyes quiver while he searched hers for something. Then he smiled, his stomach growled again and the bars of his uncanny stare broke. He was a little boy again.

When he let go of her hands, the vegetable coins were gone. 'This is for me,' he said and popped the smallest of the carrot slices into his mouth. 'The rest is for the others.' A chorus of giggles played an ensemble on the wind-strings above them.

'Look at your hands,' Wynter said as he hopped into the tree.

Eulalie looked at her still outstretched, open hands. 'They're empty,' she said. It was obvious, but true.

'Yes they are,' he said from a low branch. 'But now they're open for receiving.' He was swallowed up by the leaves. The rustling stopped and his voice snuck between the shadows. 'Don't hide your scars, because when you do, you're also hiding your stars. And they must shine. That's what stars are for. And scars. They make people who matter focus more on the shiny parts of you.'

A branch shook. Eulalie smiled and breeze rustled the leaves. She thought she heard Wynter say, 'Remember the shell I gave you. And be careful. There are monsters out there.' But it could just have been the flickering candles colluding with the breeze.

Eulalie blinked. Above her everything became suddenly quiet. The boy appeared to have vanished into thin air. If it wasn't for the shell she had in her pocket, she might have thought that she had imagined it all.

Eulalie picked up her belongings and set off again. But she didn't pull her cap lower over her eyes, she pushed it back. Kahenna's gentle fingers immediately touched her cheeks. The moon didn't appear to mind her scars. Her heart smiled.

Next stop, Lancaster Gate.

EIGHT
YOU KNOW I DON'T LIKE SPIDERS

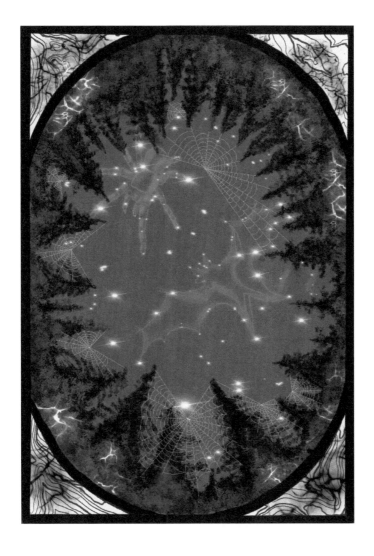

'There truly *are* monsters out there,' Eulalie said and gaped at the landscape around her. The tendons in her neck fluttered and tightened as she tried to swallow. Lancaster Gate was very different to the last time she had been there.

What at first appeared to be a low hanging bank of cotton mist swaying and drifting through the trees, was in actual fact spider webs. Enormous webs. Everywhere. Stretching from branch to branch, these terrifying traps stretched like silk-woven bridges between trees. Some spanned high up in the canopies, where they swayed in the wind like the sails of a ship, while others were lower down, expertly camouflaged, blending into the gaps between shadows.

Is this what Wynter warned me about? she thought and took a step back. Her skin crawled as she imagined eight, slow stepping hairy legs moving up her thigh. She slapped her leg. Her whole body was writhing in the power of her imagination.

'They're everywhere,' she said softly, needing to hear a voice, even if it was just her own. Her words sounded mouse-pitched and out-of-place. *Where is Spookasem?*

Eulalie urged her hearing as far away from her as possible as the drumming in chest made it impossible to hear if one of those spiders was sneaking up on her. She had walked right into a world of webs, an arachnid ambush, a sticky snag. But *where* were all the spiders?

The fallen tree that she and Spookasem had dubbed Lancaster Gate, lay about fifty paces in front of her. Its enormous root-end lay right in the middle of the path facing her, with the trunk and crumbling canopy covering the old footpath. The tree must once have been enormous as the root formed a wall as large as a house, plastered in ivy and painted in moss.

Hollow all the way through, it was quicker and far less prickly to go through the trunk, rather than wrestle the bushes on either side of it. A rusty, noisy little gate on untidy hinges lay hidden under a drapery of ferns at the entrance to this enchanted tunnel.

A carpet of honeycomb shadows cast by the clouds of webs stretched all the way from where she was standing right to the gate.

Eulalie leapt back when a shadowy clump suddenly quivered at her feet. She ducked as if a shadow-spider had thrown a net over her. If she hadn't been chewing on her lip at that moment, she would have screamed.

When nothing sticky actually got draped over her, she carefully stretched up and looked at the canopy above. The red curve of Kahenna stared at her through the lattice of web that blanketed the gap between the large trees. It almost appeared as if the moon had been captured in a net as she danced between the trees. Eulalie wished that she could take some of the web home. With it she and Spookasem might actually be able to catch shooting stars. For a moment she contemplated climbing a tree to see if she could reach one of the lower-hanging webs, when the shadow shivered again.

'Is there something stuck up there?' Eulalie whispered. She stepped off the path and craned her neck to try to spot the unfortunate creature.

An unexpected grip clamped onto her shoulder. Eulalie screamed and whirled around, lashing her hand at her attacker.

'Spookasem, I could've died,' she shouted and gasped for the air that had left her lungs.

'Wh-t do you mea- I'm th- One wh- doesn't -ike spid-'
Spookasem looked like a ghost. Not that Eulalie had ever seen one
before, but her yellow fairy tale book was full of them. Her Inkling
friend was flickering in and out of existence like a hiccup come to
life. It hurt her eyes to look at him. Not only did he vibrate, but he
seemed slightly see-through – almost like a murky pond. Eulalie
flinched and looked away, when she thought she caught a glimpse
of his intestines. Peeking back, she realised what she had thought
were his guts containing his last meal, were in actual fact just the
brambles behind him shining through.

'What? What did you say?' Eulalie kept her lips close
together when she spoke, just in case her heart jumped out of her
mouth.

Spookasem rolled his eyes and looked at the palm of his
hand. Eulalie turned her head to see his hand too.

'No, not mine, y…' Once again, his voice disappeared.

'Oh…oh. Sorry,' she said when realisation struck her.
Eulalie didn't even have to look at the fading dot of ink on her
hand. Giving him her best smile – a sheepish blend between
empathy and guilt, she fished the bottle of ink from her pocket.
She shook it, pulled the cork with her teeth and dabbed the back
of her hand on the cork. Moments later it was stoppered again and
back in her pocket.

Spookasem flickered and then re-established himself in the
air. He cupped his fringe, then rubbed his nails on his lapel before
clearing his throat.

Eulalie cleared her throat too.

She bit her lip and put her hands behind her back.

'What I meant to say,' Spookasem's voice was barely a

whisper, 'is that *I* am the one who is afraid of spiders, and *not* you.'

Eulalie swallowed hard. She couldn't look him in the eye, so she looked at her feet – her Swamp-Trotters were unrecognisable, clothed in sticky mud and something smelly.

'It moved!' Spookasem screamed when he caught sight of the shadowy clump on the ground between them.

Eulalie didn't know that Inklings could fly. The way Spookasem flapped his arms, she almost expected him to lift off.

His crash-landing in her arms verified that Inklings couldn't, in fact, fly. It was a swamp-miracle that they didn't end up in a puddle of mud or worse – a web. Somehow Eulalie managed to hold him up without dropping her lantern stick. The light swayed so violently that they were swooped on by a murder of shadows from all sides.

'It's not … at your feet. It's… above… you…' Eulalie's words wavered under the Inkling's weight.

'What? Now you tell me?' The Inkling squealed and slapped at the spiders that his imagination had slipped down his collar.

This time, they *did* end up in the mud.

*

'A shadow? You made me jump for a shadow?' Spookasem asked and was about to check his fringe with a cupped hand, but the mud in his palm convinced him otherwise. Eulalie had left him there in his puddle of shame and moved this way and that, craning her neck to find the unfortunate creature high above them.

'There…there. I think I can see it. Definitely some sort of animal,' Eulalie said. Without taking her eyes off the web's prisoner, she propped her lantern stick against the tree and angled it so that the light could chase off as many shadows as possible. Her lips moved as if she was making calculations. 'So…our plan worked?' She asked as an afterthought.

'Plan? Oh, yes. *That* plan. Worked fine. The chickens did great. Anyway. Shouldn't be out here when those spiders come out. Let's go.' He took Eulalie's stick and started marching *away* from Lancaster Gate. He couldn't hear Eulalie's footsteps - instead he heard a branch break.

'You're not considering going up there?' he asked when he turned and saw her testing a low branch of the tree that led straight up to the web. 'Seriously, Freckles. We *know* there's something up there. We can *see* that quite clearly. What are you planning to do? Check on the spider's supper to make sure that it's nutritious enough?'

'Gonna save it,' she said while using some large toadstools attached to the tree as stepping stones to reach the first bough. Each fungus on the higher boughs puffed fireflies of spores each time one of Eulalie's large Swamp-Trotters stamped on it.

'What?' Spookasem slapped his own forehead, this time not caring about upsetting his quiff. 'What in the names of the four moons for? It's spider food. A *monster* has caught another *monster*; frankly, we're better off for it. One less creature to worry about.' He put the stick against the tree again.

He stomped right under the branch Eulalie was balancing on. 'Come on down and we can talk about this sensibly. Why save one puny little creature? By the look of these webs, half the swamp will be eaten by morning…even us. Saving one won't make the slightest difference at all.' He folded his arms.

That last statement got Eulalie's attention. Hunched over between two branches, she looked at the Inkling. Her eyes bored into his. 'It'll make a difference to *that* one up there,' she said. And just like that, the Inkling was silenced. He took up his position as lookout, and even helped guide Eulalie to the best hand and footholds he could see from where he was standing.

NINE
SURPRISE PACKAGE

If there was one thing that Eulalie knew that she was good at, it was climbing trees. It didn't take her long to get close enough to take a better look.

'I don't know what it is. Totally cocooned in the web,' Eulalie said. She had become just another shadow among a leafy ocean of many. 'Just... a ... little... bit... further...' Eulalie gritted her teeth and stretched as far as her body could go, but she still wasn't close enough to touch the captive. The branch beneath her bent like a bow and groaned a warning that it wasn't going to be able to hold her weight much longer. A fall from such a dizzying height would most certainly mean the end of her.

'Darn it,' Eulalie sighed and shuffled back to the trunk. The knotted bundle shook and hissed as if reminding her that it was still alive and that Eulalie shouldn't leave it there. 'Sshhhh, little one, shhhh. I'll have you out in no time,' she said to it.

Despite the icy bite of the air so high up, Eulalie was dripping with sweat. She bit her lip. Sometimes perilous situations required perilous decisions.

'Spook, Spook,' she called out, mind made up.

'Have you got it yet?' He tried to whisper his shout, but his voice still carried further than he intended it to.

'No, not yet. I need you to do something for me,' Eulalie called.

Spookasem's heart sank. He could already pick up a hint of an apology in her voice as if there was an inevitability of imminent disaster. 'I'm not climbing up there...' he called out.

'No. No. I need you to keep a close eye on this web. I'm gonna have to slide along the silk to get close enough to free the little animal. The branches won't hold my weight,' she said.

'Are you … Are you mad!' It wasn't actually a question, but a brutally honest statement hidden *behind* a flimsy question. 'You'll get stuck.' He blinked something out of his eye. 'And how do you know it's an animal? It might be the spider's baby all snuggly wrapped up in a webby blanket. Did you hear me? You'll get stuck. Webs are sticky.'

'I won't. Spiders don't make the edges of their webs sticky; so, they can climb their own webs. But my movement is gonna bring the spider out. I need you to warn me when it comes.' she whisper-called.

'And then? What will you do then?' Spookasem drenched his words in dread.

'Don't worry, just keep an eye out for me. I have a plan.' Eulalie didn't lie. She *did* have a plan. It wasn't a clever one, but it was a plan. If the spider *did* decide to come out, she'd have to jump for a cluster of branches not too far below her. It might just break her fall. Anyway – she was committed to the little prisoner now. There was no turning back.

Eulalie reached for the place where the web attached to the tree and tapped the rope-like strand. Yip, just as she thought – not sticky. It felt strange, though – nothing like she imagined – but then again, she had never touched such a big web before.

Grasping onto the strand above her head, she stepped onto the one below. She was shaking so much that the spider was most probably going to come out before she even got to the little thing out there. Leaning back and allowing the web to take her full weight, Eulalie shuffled out between the trees.

'Blessed moons. Blessed moons,' Spookasem said. His

stomach lurched on Eulalie's behalf and it felt to him as if he had swallowed a handful of fluttering butterflies.

'Don't look down,' Eulalie whispered to try and silence the voice that kept on telling her to look down. She looked down. 'Watch out,' she called to the Inkling below when her hat slipped off her head. 'One, two, three, four, five, six…'

'Ouch. My eye,' Spookasem answered.

'Sorry. I warned you. Good news,' Eulalie called.

'Do you have it?' he asked.

'No. It only took six counts for my hat to reach you. If I fall I might survive,' Eulalie said. She actually sounded cheerful at that thought.

Spookasem sighed in exasperation. 'If you didn't hear that, I sighed in exasperation,' he shouted. 'Sometimes I think it would be best to put a leash on that girl,' he said to himself.

'Ok, not far now.' Eulalie's knuckles turned white; her fingers cramped and ached and her arms were beginning to shake. She'd have to rest once she got close to the captive.

The closer she got to the little entangled bundle, the more it shook. It was either very excited that Eulalie was so close, or it was terrified that Eulalie was perhaps the spider.

'It's ok. I'm here to help,' she said when she finally reached it. She stopped with the knotty bundle between her hands. It immediately stopped struggling. Playing dead maybe.

'Now for some web acrobatics. *Webrobatics* I'll call it,' she chuckled at her own joke. 'Spook. I've invented a new word. *Webrobatics*!' she called to the Inkling.

Spookasem slapped his forehead and shook his head.

Eulalie slid her fingers along the cross-fibres of the web

that she hadn't touched yet. 'Strange. Not sticky either,' she said. Relieved that she wouldn't get stuck, she dangled her elbows over the strand to free up her hands. At first a cramp, then relief flooded her knotted fingers.

'What are you?' Eulalie asked after her fingers had stopped shivering and she could inspect the bundle. 'You're *not* cocooned up. Just terribly entangled. If I can just move this ...and shift that ...and pull that one aside, then I can free your face.'

Large bulging eyes popped open as Eulalie freed the creature's face. Half-a-heartbeat later it snapped at her with razor pearly teeth.

'Whaoh. Careful.' Eulalie ripped her hand back and her arm slid free from her own safety-tangle. One moment she was standing – the next she was dangling by one hand.

'Watch out,' Spookasem screamed.

'Duck,' Eulalie shouted when her toes couldn't cling onto a boot any longer and it plummeted to the swampy floor. Thankfully Eulalie was far too busy trying to swing herself back onto her earlier perch to hear the Inkling's curses when the boot landed on his face.

Back in position and re-entangled, Eulalie found herself face to face with the strangest animal she had ever seen. It was about the size of a large, ripe avocado – and she had climbed many a tree for those before - but never this high.

The creature dropped its menacing look when it appeared to realise that the peculiar freckled girl wasn't going to eat it. And despite its disastrous entanglement, every part of its face appeared to work together to form a smile. Lines and troughs of a puppy frown rippled between bulging walnut eyes; worm-like eye-brows pulled and pushed at turret-ears as though they were marionettes on strings. A wreck of whiskers vibrated as its black lips pulled into an upturned sickle moon. Framed by forever-lashes, its unblinking eyes burned into Eulalie's soul. A petite, cat-like nose swivelled as it sniffed the air. Its teeth didn't seem half as menacing now that its mouth was framed in friendliness.

'What are you, little one?' Eulalie whispered. Its bat-like ears turned and twitched when Eulalie spoke. There was something familiar about it, but Eulalie just couldn't put her finger on it. She'd seen something like it before. 'Now don't struggle. Let me help you.' Eulalie reached for it again.

The little creature started struggling again. It pawed at her with cub-claws, hind legs scraping. Then, as it tried to flap a pair of heavily entangled leathery wings, it whined and instantly stopped it's fight with the web. In that moment, Eulalie realised what it was.

'Spook, Spookasem, I know what it is. I've seen one in my brown fairy-tale book on a picture of that cathedral. It's a gargoyle. A gargoyle.' She nearly lost her grip in her excitement.

'I think you should hurry up,' was the Inkling's answer. Eulalie might be doing the *Webrobatics*, but his own situation had suddenly taken a dangerous turn too.

'Nearly there. Nearly there,' Eulalie said. 'Don't struggle. Your wing's broken. Almost. There. Don't. Struggle. Gotcha. Spook. I've got it.'

Once Eulalie had the gargoyle pup cradled in her arm, she suddenly realised that she hadn't come up with a plan of how to get down using only one arm. She didn't have to contemplate that for long. The gargoyle pup kicked itself free and escaped Eulalie's tender grasp.

'No...No, Spook catch. Its wing's broken!' she screamed.

'Eulalie. You'd better hurry, we've got a problem down here...Whaoh!'

Spookasem's legs slid left as his body went right. He floundered for a moment, and just as it seemed he would regain control of his confused legs, he toppled backwards. Hopefully for the last time that night, something landed on top of him.

'Freckles, I've caught it. I've caught it. And it's alive,' the Inkling shouted, his voice was sunrise and sugar all in one.

TEN
RUMBLE AND RUN

'You did it,' Eulalie called. She half-tumbled, half-bounced from branch to branch to reach the ground. Bounding from an impossibly high perch, she landed cat-like in a swamp puddle that exploded in a muddy rainbow around her. 'You're the best,' she exclaimed and flung her arms around the Inkling's neck.

'Uhm…Eulalie,' the Inkling swung the gargoyle out of the way to prevent it from becoming a sandwich between them. 'I think you need to…'

'Look.' Eulalie interrupted him. She pulled away and stroked the gargoyle's head. Her fingers were still shivering from her climb.

The Inkling tried again. 'Eulalie. If you could just stop that for a moment and…'

'I see. It's wing's definitely broken.' Eulalie knew all about bumps and bruises. The lines and furrows on the little guy's face expressed all too well how she had felt too many times before.

'Look behind you,' Spookasem said.

Eulalie swung around. 'Ah, yes. Thanks,' she said. 'That branch is perfect for a splint. We'll have to take it home until its healed. We could call it *Toktokki*. No. Maybe not. I think it's a boy. Rudolf. His name is Rudolf. We can hide him in my room. Or one of the attics – the one close to the Wishing Willow tree. Lots of beams to dangle upside down from. Do you think gargoyles dangle? Looks kind of bat-like to me…' Eulalie was quite beside herself with excitement.

'Eulalie. By the moons. Keep quiet. Turn around and look between the …two… large… trees,' Spookasem whispered. If his hands weren't cradling a baby gargoyle, he would have taken her by the shoulders and *helped* her turn. That's when Eulalie realised that Spookasem hadn't been looking at the gargoyle or her at all, but over her shoulder at something behind.

She turned following his gaze. And froze. 'There's something there,' Eulalie said, her voice barely a rustle.

Two bright yellow eyes stared at them from the nest of shadows in the undergrowth.

'That's what I've been trying to tell you. I think it's a spider,' Spookasem said. His heart pounded like raindrops on sand.

'No. They have eight,' Eulalie said. She had lowered her voice to a hum. 'And by the way. You're an Inkling. You're invisible. Nothing is supposed to be able to s...' She swallowed her last words when she noticed that the gargoyle pup, lying in Spookasem's arms, was gazing straight up at him, thereby hurling the invisible Inkling theory out of the window.

The gargoyle pup whimpered.

In an explosion of leaves, snapping twigs and breaking branches, the owner of the yellow eyes charged.

A curtain of shadows were ripped in two and a larger, very much larger version of the gargoyle known as Rudolf, materialised out of the dark. Head held low like a charging wolf, the adult gargoyle scrambled towards them. Its mast-like wings bent forwards, claws ripping into the muddy soil as it propelled itself forwards. Shrubs splintered beneath its weight and nettles were torn up and scattered. Abruptly it stopped about five paces from them; stooped and ready to spring, its wings peaked like gigantic half-open umbrellas. Slowly it spread its wings wide like open sails, then plunged its wing-claws into the ground and roared. Its neck disappeared under waves of muscles and bulging veins as its booming voice burnt the air.

Spookasem squealed.

Eulalie inhaled a scream, her hands searching for the Inkling behind her.

Rudolf gulped and gurgled.

The large gargoyle lifted itself onto its leopard legs, bullied the air with its front claws as it arched its back, towering above Eulalie and Spookasem. In a final demonstration of its ferocity, it hissed and slammed its claws into mud that splattered everywhere, finishing with a whip-like crack of its wings that severed all warmth from the air.

'Spook. Don't move.' Eulalie urged the Inkling. 'I think it's Rudolf's momma.'

'I *know*. What should I do? Take him…should I …give him back?' Spookasem asked. Only a few crumbs of what he tried to say wafted into Eulalie's direction.

'Give Rudolf to me.' Still keeping her eyes on mother gargoyle, Eulalie reached for the baby. Mother Rudolf responded by raising her upper lip. Rows of razor fangs verified that she didn't like anyone reaching for her young.

'Maybe…' Spook tried to say.

'… that wasn't such a good idea,' Eulalie finished his sentence and dropped her hands. 'I think *you* should take Rudolf back to her. I've got a plan.'

Spookasem's heart sank. Eulalie's plans were frequently scarred with flaws; now was not a good time to patch up Eulalie's tapestry of moth-eaten ideas.

'Eulalie. Shouldn't we rather think ab…' Spookasem's voice had turned ashen.

'Don't worry, Spook. If the mother attacks you, I'll rub out your ink,' Eulalie said. Her own fear was well masked in a thin layer of confidence.

Spookasem breathed in a counter-argument, but it took just a moment for the idea to find root. He had to admit that it was actually *not* such a bad idea.

'Shhh, now little one…Rudolf I mean. Easy now Rudolf,' Spook shushed the pup while patting him on his head. He edged past Eulalie. 'Keep an eye on that freckle. Make sure you rub at the *correct* one,' he said to Eulalie, before turning his attention to yellow-eyes. 'Hello, mother. What lovely yellow eyes you have…all the better to scare us children with.' Spookasem was hoping that the mother gargoyle wouldn't perceive his shaking legs as an act of aggression.

The mother gargoyle stole a step closer too. It was mind-boggling to see something that was supposed to be carved out of stone and attached to the gutters of buildings, in actual flesh and blood.

'Be careful,' Eulalie said.

'There, now Rudolf. Mummy's here,' Spookasem said and lifted him towards his mother. The poor creature's injured wing swung limp like one of the broken sails of the old mill.

Some of the aggression lines on the mother gargoyle's face pulled smooth, leaving a slightly friendlier visage – but one that was still masked with cautionary shadows. She squinted her yellow eyes and for the first time since the Inkling had spied them in the shadows, she released him from her gaze and turned her eyes to her baby.

Instantly a veil of fuzziness dropped over her and she

cocked her head to the side.

'Come now. Take him,' the Inkling bit down onto his teeth to prevent them from clattering together.

'Spook. You're doing fine,' Eulalie said.

'You're going to owe me *big time* for this,' he whispered over his shoulder and Eulalie gulped an answer.

Rudolf purred cat-like, scrubbed his ear into Spookasem's hand and then reached for his mother.

Everyone froze.

It started as a vibration – a deep hum that hung heavy in the air. Eulalie felt her insides tickle, then shake and then she had to clasp her hands to her ears as a piercing bellow sliced through the trees and ripped the shadows apart.

The mother gargoyle snatched the baby from Spookasem. Her wings slapped the air, knocking the Inkling out of the way and she took flight, barely avoiding the web above them.

'Spook, Spook,' Eulalie tried to force her voice past the terrible sound. 'What's... what's going on?'

'What in the names of the four moons...' the Inkling's lips formed the words, but he couldn't hear them spoken. Even after the wail had died away, its echo remained, imprinted in the mist, scraped into the cold air and etched into all the free space around them.

Eulalie was still crouched down, her hands fast on her ears. It felt to Eulalie as if the ground was about to split open.

Spookasem put his little finger into his own and shook it, trying to loosen the high-pitched hiss stuck inside. He steadied himself against the trunk of a tree.

'Hun...hunt...hunters,' Eulalie said and stood up, her eyes

wide with terror as the realisation dawned on her. 'Hunters. That was a hunter's bellow. Marauders. Red Marauders are coming. They charge into the crimson night and kill everything they see.'

A shadow flew over them, followed by another, then another.

Something flew into the web above them in a dull thud.

'No,' Eulalie and Spookasem said together.

'That rumbling. It's a stampede.' Eulalie whispered. She picked up her hat and pulled at the strap of her bag.

'I think now's a good time to run,' Spook answered and spun around.

'Quick. Lancaster Gate. Run for the gate,' Eulalie shouted and followed, her legs moving so fast that it felt as if her upper body couldn't quite keep up.

ELEVEN
LANCASTER GATE

'Eulalie? Freckles?' Spookasem's voice sounded strangely muffled by the moss and fern-covered walls inside Lancaster Gate. Clouds of vapour ghosts clung to his lips with every gasping breath. The pitter patter of hundreds of tiny footsteps drizzled in a panicked stampede across the roof of the log of wood.

'Shhhhh,' came her response. More pin-like footsteps followed. A terrified, bell-like voice called out from the entrance of the hollowed log. An answer chimed like an alarm bell.

'Quick, give me that,' Eulalie said.

The Inkling snatched up their lantern and handed it to her. Without a moment's delay, she scramble-crawled back to the entrance, holding the light in front of her. Splinters in palm and scratches on knees later, she was crouching at the rusty gate. The tinkling came from the outside.

'Come in. It's fine. We won't harm you.' Eulalie whispered. She couldn't see what she was talking to, but there was a rustling in the brambles mere inches from her. A tremble of high, clear bells rang. She glimpsed a peculiar shadow – thin arms, pointy ears. 'Maybe you don't like the light,' she said. 'Spook, sit still. Whatever happens, don't move,' she whispered over her shoulder.

'Why does it feel as if the floor just opened up beneath me?' the Inkling asked himself.

Eulalie blew out the flame. A smoke-spirit tumbled, pirouetted and contorted on the still-red ember of the wick like a macabre ballerina on a music box. The leaves at the entrance of their hide-out shook and a flurry of activity wrestled with the undergrowth. Guided by nothing but the dim glow of Kahenna's light that filtered through the trees, Eulalie moved some of the nettles aside. Red-hot needles burnt her fingers where she touched the leaves. She held on, though. Something hopped onto her arm and over her shoulder. Another followed. Eulalie heard Spookasem squirm as he, too, was trampled on by those tiny feet. When she was certain that there was no-one else stuck outside, she reached out and pulled a small branch of dead leaves across the entrance and crawled back to the Inkling.

'What *were* those things? I swear they were running on two legs,' Spookasem asked. He tried to sound more curious than scared.

'Dunno. Couldn't see them clearly,' Eulalie answered. The little shadows had, however, reminded her of a picture in one of her fairy-tale books.

'Freckles,' Spookasem said after a moment. 'I've got your
. . .'

'Shhhh, I hear something.' The ember on the candle-wick blinked and finally went out, releasing its hold on the tail of the smoke. Ghost-like it hovered in gossamer filaments as if afraid of its unexpected freedom.

Incoherent voices sounded in the distance, warped as if spoken under water. People were shouting and someone laughed. Eulalie urged her hearing to make out what the voices were saying, but the thumping of her heart didn't give her a chance. 'I think they're the Marauders,' she said.

'Freckles, I've got your boot. Picked it up as we ran,' Spookasem whispered.

'Thanks Spook,' Eulalie answered. 'That was very kind, but you shouldn't have been thinking of rescuing a boot for me. Our lives were at stake.'

A slight expectant pressure filled their perfect darkness.

Spookasem cleared his throat. 'I…uhm…didn't. I picked it up as a weapon. Thought that either the smell or its projectile properties might come in handy,' he replied and blindly waved the boot out in front of him hoping that Eulalie would take it from him.

'Freckles?' he suddenly asked and shuffled right into Eulalie. Thousands of goosepimples rushed uninvited from the backs of his legs, right up to the top of his head. He breathed in, out, in, out, in…and then held his breath.

'What now? There are people right outside the gate. I'm trying to listen what they're up to,' Eulalie said.

'Sorry, but this is an emergency. Is your hair hanging loose or is the mop tied up?' Spookasem asked.

'I'm wearing a hat,' she answered.

'Oh.'

The silence that followed was unnerving. Eulalie felt Spookasem's body tense up, almost shiver where it pressed against her.

'Then, just to make sure,' he finally said, 'this hairy clump that is moving across the back of my neck couldn't be your hair?' He didn't wait for an answer.

'Spook. Spook.' Somehow Eulalie managed to avoid his flailing arms and legs and a random flying boot without too many new bruises and grasped his wrist. 'Calm down. Look. Light.'

The Inkling stopped kicking, but his breathing still rasped and whistled in an oven of curses.

'Shhhhh,' she nearly dropped on top of him to get her warning to his ear. 'Look. Light.'

Tentative to creep into this mysterious tree stump, a quivering wave of light stretched out towards them, stopping inches from their feet. Eulalie curled her knees up to her chin to prevent the light from finding her. Someone had found the entrance Eulalie had tried to conceal. Whoever it was, was holding up a lantern and was trying to peek into the tree trunk. His shadow seeped into the light, coiled and danced like ink dropped into water.

Eulalie and Spookasem held their breaths. Together, their heartbeats sounded like a second stampede. Eulalie put her hand to her chest, trying to muffle the drumming.

'Definitely went in here. I saw one. Running on two legs, I swear,' a voice weighed down by a strange accent said. It desecrated their silence, tainting it with the excitement of the hunt. He must have been running, because his breathing was hard and deep. Eulalie could just make out the ghosts of water vapour forming at the mouth of his silhouette against the distant entrance.

'Yes. I saw it too. Most probably some sort of large ape. Go to the other end of the log, you fool,' another voice said. Their shadows thickened as they joined together at the entrance.

'No chance am I climbing through those brambles. They'll rip me to shreds,' the first answered.

Eulalie knew exactly what the stranger was talking about. A wall of brambles grew over and on either side of the log. The only quick way to get to the other side was through the log – it would take you at least half a turn of an hourglass to go around the thicket and backbreaking labour to hack your way through the thorns – if you even happened to have something sharp enough; though the Marauders probably did.

'Then go through, you coward.' The second sounded like quite a bully. If it wasn't for his accent, it might as well have been

Eulalie's brother.

'Me? Why me? You go. Who knows what manner of creature crawled in there. Meet one of the freakish beasts who live in this strange moon's light in a confined space? No thanks. I'd rather swim with sharks.' The first was adamant. He was not crawling in.

'Eulalie? What's *sharks*?' the Inkling asked.

'I don't know, Spook, but...'

'Look. Look what I've found,' one of the Marauders interrupted her. His outline stooped and picked something up.

A moment later something tugged at Eulalie's thigh.

'He's pulling the line, Spookasem,' Eulalie said while trying to lift her hips to free herself from the entanglement. 'He's found my blue line. And I'm sitting on this end.'

'It's stuck,' the first Marauder said. The line pulled again. This time even harder. 'There's something attached to the end of this.'

'Yank it,' the second said.

More pulling ensued. The light continued its exploring. Shadows ran for cover.

'Eulalie. Look. That's what crawled on me,' was all Spookasem could get out of his lungs. The rest of his words drowned in shock and terror.

Right at the edge of the light, doing a slow, methodical tightrope between the light and the dark, balanced the shadow of enormous spider. A hand's width from Spookasem's boots – and Eulalie's bootless foot – its long, hairy legs stretched on the line of shadow as if stuck in treacle. There was no-where for Eulalie to go – and it was probably a good thing that Spookasem was hugging so tight into her, else her heart would most probably have burst out of her chest.

'There's definitely still something in there. Listen,' one of the men said. The Marauder shadows turned their heads towards Eulalie and Spookasem; they held their breaths. The spider didn't – it appeared to inspect Eulalie's big toe that was sticking out of a very frayed hole in her sock. Its front legs lifted and stroked a dangling thread.

'Spook,' she cringed.

'Eulalie,' Spookasem squirmed.

Boots crunched and twigs snapped at the little gate. One of the Marauders spoke. 'Well, if you're not going to do something about it, then move out of my way.' The tugging at the string stopped as the first Marauder's shadow pulled away, leaving the taller, older looking one alone in the light. A series of strange sounds followed. Half keeping her eye on the spider and the shadow, Eulalie was trying to put the puzzle of his movements together. It was only when the man stretched his arms, accompanied by the moan of wood being strained, that she realised what was about to happen.

'Sp… arrow,' was all Eulalie could get out, before the bow coughed, spitting out the arrow. No time for them to move, both merely blinked.

TWELVE
ARROWS AND INK

The arrow thunked right next to Eulalie's head, bits of wood and splinters raining onto her. It had passed right between Eulalie and Spookasem. When she moved forwards, her cheek pressed into its unfriendly shaft.

'Eulalie. Rub out the ink. I'll have to distract them,' Spookasem said. His urgent fingers dug into her shoulder.

The bow groaned and spat again. Another arrow barely missed them. Eulalie felt the air clasp her cheek as the shadows dived for cover. This arrow bounced and clattered somewhere behind them.

'Eulalie, rub out the ink. Count to ten and then put the ink back. I'll appear a few paces from here, hopefully not in the brambles on either side of this trunk. I can distract them.' Spookasem's voice was like a rush of water.

'Curses,' the Marauder firing the arrows swore. 'Missed. I can still hear something move in there.'

'Eulalie. Now,' Spookasem said.

'Ok. Ok,' Eulalie said. She licked the back of her hand and rubbed it with the other.

'Wrong hand,' Spook said. 'You're not even touching it yet. Hurry. I think I can hear the bow groan again.'

Eulalie licked the other, tasted the ink and rubbed it. 'Be careful...' she said and moments later she felt the emptiness that always followed when her Inkling disappeared. Then she ducked, expecting another hungry arrow to be hunting her down.

'Don't shoot. I've a better plan,' a Marauder said, 'Come. Follow me.' The light pulled back, ripping the Marauder's shadow with it. Moments later footsteps echoed onto the wood above her. In such a confined space their stamping feet sounded more like boulders rolling down a mountain.

'Ten. Surely that's more than ten counts now,' Eulalie whispered to herself. Her hand plunged into her pocket. Icy fingers of dread gripped her chest. Her other hand dug into the other pocket. 'No.' The bottle of ink was missing. 'Spook. No. No. No,' Eulalie repeated while crawling on all fours, searching for the lost bottle of ink. Dread, shock and loss weighed heavier on her than the threat of hunters and their arrows. In the dark, her hands found bits of rotten wood, fern-like stems and the soggy, sliminess of squashed mushrooms - and her boot.

Eulalie pressed her back against the wall and slipped her boot back on. 'Spookasem. My dear Spookasem. What should I do?' she asked. Her voice quivered and she had to blink the welling tears away before they blinded her even more in the already-dark.

Her eyes moved to the black ceiling above her. The footsteps that had moments earlier appeared to magically follow her movements had also stopped. Something shifted, the log creaked. Silence followed. It was a holding-of-a-breath silence – one that was stretched tight like a piece of elastic. It couldn't hold for long. She had to do something.

It was difficult to judge exactly how deep she was down the trunk. If she managed to move further along, sooner or later, the Marauders would have to start battling the brambles that were also growing on top of the log if they wanted to follow her. The undergrowth wasn't as thick as it was at the sides, but it would slow them down and give them some good scratches, she hoped. Eulalie shifted around. Her back nudged into her bag of presents.

Momentarily she thought of pushing the sack out in front

of her, but then she decided that it would be quicker if she slung it over her shoulder – a decision that saved her life.

She had just settled back onto all fours, about to crawl deeper down the log, when the first arrow slammed through her tree-trunk-roof.

Eulalie screamed. The thickness of the trunk had slowed it down, but it still managed to slice into the bag that was now protecting most of her back. One of the presents took the brunt of the force, but Eulalie was still left half-pinned to the rotten carpet of swamp sludge on the log floor.

Lying flat on her face, she composed a most wonderful solo of words that would have made pirates blush. Without holding back, she shared it with the bitter decomposition her lips were stuck to. Those poisonous words somehow filled her with enough strength to yank herself free.

A thin ray of quivering orange burned through the hole the arrow left behind. 'By the blessings of the four moons,' she hissed. 'What are they shooting with?'

The moment she started crawling, another arrow followed. 'Aaargh! Rot-and-grot,' Eulalie hissed and grabbed her forehead. The arrow had snuck through her hat. The tip had missed her skin, but the shaft had knocked her forehead. 'My hat, now I've got to patch it up,' she complained with her finger wriggling through the damage. She slapped it back onto her head with a grunt, ignoring the throbbing just above her brow that would most probably swell like an egg in less than half a turn.

Eulalie crawled on, her hands slapping into the tree-floor with renewed energy. Behind her more thuds followed. She lost count how many. She paused once, grazed hands and knees throbbing, to look back. Lines of amber light criss-crossed where at least half a dozen arrows had ripped through the old tree-trunk tunnel. If the situation hadn't turned so sour, she might actually have stopped for longer to admire the effect. It looked pretty, almost encouraging with the light-fingers crossed to bring her good luck.

Only a few paces on, it was as if Eulalie had crawled over an invisible barrier that the arrows couldn't cross. More lines of bleeding light joined the others, but the holes had stopped following her. The Marauders, of course, had been stopped by a wall – one with leaves that burnt with invisible fire and stems covered with their own little arrows that pointed their unfriendly bits in all directions.

'I'll never complain about brambles again,' Eulalie whispered and rushed to the silhouetted outlines of thin, twiggy arms and leafy fingers that marked the exit to Lancaster Gate.

Eulalie eyed the gate of brambles. 'I hope you don't mind me asking just to show a bit of mercy…please. I've just escaped becoming a pin-cushion and I would appreciate it if it could stay this way.' The brambles didn't answer; they didn't look any less threatening either.

'Well, at least there seems to be a little path leading through you,' she said, hoping that it wasn't her imagination painting a path of hope with a brush dipped in wishful thinking.

Eulalie pulled her hat down as far as it would go, accepting the fact that there was no negotiating with brambles.

Stooped over, she let out a long moan. Lifting her high collar even higher, she nuzzled her neck and chin into its protective lining.

'I'm going to regret this in the morning,' she caught up with her moan and together, they rushed into the brambles.

*

A tiny spider, barely bigger than a mosquito, dropped off the back of Eulalie's gift-pack, having decided that the dark was a better option than the brambles. It scuttled over to a little hole in the rotten tree, reminiscing about how enormous its shadow had looked earlier when it was dancing on the barrier between the light and the dark.

*

Eulalie darted from shadow to shadow, making sure her boots found patches of grass instead of mud and despite their size and weight, they whispered rather than splashed. 'Won't stop them following me,' she said to herself. 'But hopefully slow them down.'

With her legs wobbling and every inch of her exposed skin scratched and torn by the brambles, Eulalie approached Knightsbridge.

THIRTEEN
INTO THE JAWS OF KNIGHTSBRIDGE

Out of all of the places labelled on her and Spookasem's *London Underground Mind the Gap Map* they had managed to discover and explore so far, Knightsbridge had been most aptly named. It appeared to have tumbled from one of Eulalie's fairy-tale books and was a very special place to her. It was one of those places where reality and imagination wed in a glorious ceremony of wonder and mystery.

What must have once been an enormous statue that would have towered above the trees and been visible for miles, now lay in ruins before her, almost completely reclaimed by the slow, methodical hands of nature. Only the statue's face, shoulder and hands remained.

Wearing a knight's helmet, most of the head and face - bearded in moss and lichen - protruded out of a grassy mound. His eyes - one now hidden behind an eye-patch of finch nests - were turned up to the sky and his mouth froze agape in what Eulalie imagined to be a heroic war cry. Spookasem had disagreed at the time– he was convinced that the knight was only yawning. The rest of the knight's body was missing, either destroyed or taken for building material. Another possibility was that it was just hidden beneath the ground, untouched and unseen; a grave draped in a shroud of ivy.

A little further down the mound, the statue's hands were clasped together as if in prayer, holding the tip of a sickle-moon. The crescent stretched like an enchanted bridge across a little stream, before plunging back into the undergrowth.

Eulalie scrambled over the knight's lower jaw and crawled into the ferns and shadows he appeared to be chewing on. This mandible-cave was dry and the walls were hard enough to withstand those deadly arrows the Marauders had fired through the trunk of Lancaster Gate.

Eulalie's legs buckled and she collapsed into the knight's tonsils. She stretched her legs out in front of her and rubbed her hands over her numb thighs. Her eyes searched the trees in the crimson light. 'Rudolf. I hope you and your momma got away safely,' she said. What would happen if he could never fly again? Would he survive? Or would the mother desert him when she realised that he wouldn't be able to keep up?

Kahenna, the crimson moon, wrapped herself in the canopy of a trees cluster as though hiding her face from the Marauders who invaded her world. The trees swayed, and it seemed as if the moon winked at her with gnarled eyelashes.

It felt strange to be there without Spookasem.

One of Eulalie and Spookasem's adventures – one that had no end in sight and blended into their daily lives – was to dig out the statue to see if it had actually fallen, or whether it was still standing and the landscape had merely grown around it. That was Eulalie's motivation for the possibly impossible task. Her boundary-less, imagination painted pictures of how the landscape rolled up, twisted, dipped and cracked millennia ago when one of the other moons, Kalani crashed into their planet. That one, dramatic, world changing moment, remembered in myth across the world must - in Eulalie's mind - have buried the statue in a wave of rock and hills, with its builders and worshippers swallowed and forgotten with it.

Spookasem was just as curious as his freckled friend about the statue, but his motivation for digging was different to hers. He just wanted to see whether the knight was wearing Swamp-

Trotters or not – and if he *was*, whether they were as big as Eulalie's.

Whatever their motivation, dig they had – eleven broken shovels, weeks of stiff legs and aching backs, blisters on palms and one broken finger later – Spookasem had trodden on Eulalie's hand – they had reached the man's armpit. It had been a triumph and a whole juicy bunch of fruit for their hard labour – they celebrated that momentous occasion with a relaxing evening on the roof of *The Cross in the Roads* trying to catch shooting stars with fishing nets. Even though Spookasem had been adamant that the burnt hole in his net had come from a shooting star he managed to snag when Eulalie wasn't looking, they had been unsuccessful at catching anything tangible. They did, however, right the world's wrongs in their plans and philosophical debates and had a barn-bundle of fun.

With life returning to her legs again, Eulalie emptied her bag. 'Where are you?' she asked. 'Maybe I put the inkwell in the bag and just can't remember doing it. Hey, what's this?' she whispered, momentarily pushing aside the constant throbbing of panic about her bottle of ink. Between the gifts lay one of the strange arrows the Marauders had fired.

Eulalie picked it up as if it could still harm her. 'Phew,' she whistled when she felt its weight in her hand. It was far thicker and shorter than any arrows she'd seen before.

Maybe it's an arrow for one of those new crossbow things that people were talking about, she thought.

Subconsciously she pushed herself deeper into the statue's mouth and her gaze circled her walls of protection. '*Surely* they couldn't shoot through this solid rock?' she asked. She tapped the short arrow against the giant's cheek. 'Surely?'

Eulalie needed a plan, a new one. 'Won't be lighting any more of you this evening, lest I give my position away,' she said as she put the candles back into her bag. 'Need to find Spookasem's ink and then try and get home. Maybe avoid being murdered along the way.' Eulalie tried to see a funny side to everything that happened so far. She struggled but forced a smile anyway. A cool breeze found its way into silent opening of the screaming-mouth cave. Her smile might not have meant that she was happy, but it showed that she was strong.

A hunter's horn suddenly raised its brass voice to the night sky. Instantly, a commotion broke out in the tree as a pigeon bludgeoned its way through the leaves. Its feathers tickled the stone giant's ear in its desperate flight. Moments later the bird's distinct whistling flutter disappeared off into the uncertain night. 'Lancaster Gate,' she whispered to the moon. 'That's where the horn sounded from. The Marauders must have found their way around it. Time to move,' she said.

Eulalie stood up and slung her duffle bag over her shoulder. For a moment she had contemplated waking her own bow and arrows from their slumber. Then she thought of how those Marauders' arrows had cut through the log, and she decided against it. There was simply no way she was going to poop the hunters into submission.

Distant movement caught her eye. Pulling whatever shadows she could borrow from the ivy and moss that was flossing the giant's mouth, she squinted into the almandine dark. Kahenna had moved and was beginning to sneak past a hillock of trees she called Shepherds Bush. A snake-like coil danced just above the tops of the trees. Grey and ominous it slithered, unnatural and out of place in Kahenna's light.

Eulalie breathed deeply. 'Smoke,' she said. The dangerous odour of smoke had bullied its way into the night's perfume of wet leaves and water puddles. The smoke smelled purposeful and cold – hardly any flames. This was not a fire for warmth, but one to steal the air from creatures where they hid and to frighten them out into the open.

Eulalie had barely swung one leg over the giant's lower jaw, when a dazzling light swung across the undergrowth, bouncing and weaving through the ferns. It was soon joined by a second circle of light that scanned the branches of a nearby tree.

FOURTEEN
PINPOINT LANTERNS

'Pinpointers. Blessed Moons. They've got pinpoint lanterns.' Eulalie cursed and cartwheeled back into the giant's mouth, keeping her head down. She was only just in time too. One of the beams of light swerved over the exact spot she had been standing only a heartbeat earlier, before gliding over her hiding place – which was the knight's lower incisors – to shine upon the back of the giant's throat.

Cli-creak, cli-creak, cli-creak.

Rusty wheels complaining, Eulalie thought. *Just please don't come too close.* Just as she thought she'd have to run, the cart sighed as it came to a halt.

'Jeepers creepers, have you ever seen such a huge statue? *Who...* or should I rather ask *what* carved that?' a now familiar voice asked. The Marauder's words seemed to corrupt Kahenna's stained-glass world.

'Hideous, if you ask me. Stop your gaping and help me with this. I'm getting nervous travelling with this quarry,' the second Marauder said. Something *clunked*, followed almost instantly by a heavy *thunk*. 'That's it. Careful now. That box's latch is broken. Watch out. I think that thing in there can bite. That's better. Keep your fingers away from the bars. Now I want these nets in place before those smoke-fires start chasing the creatures this way. The wind is perfect. Blowing straight at us.'

Eulalie angled her head and urged her hearing out into the dark. Leaves flapped like the strips of sail that dangled from her mill and some branches snapped. *What are they up to?*

And then her heart skipped a beat. Somewhere squashed between their loud, stomping steps and thick curses, Eulalie heard whimpering. 'They have Rudolf,' Eulalie said. A faceless cold rushed into the mouth-cave and clamped her heart, stifling her flames of hope.

Urging the shadows to keep her covered, she peeped over the giant's teeth…and gasped.

Two men were busying themselves spreading a large net between a couple of trees. At least, Eulalie *assumed* that they were men. She had to tear her eyes from their ghastly visages.

Instead of two eyes positioned fairly central above a small nose – as one would of course expect - *their* eyes were enormous, almost taking up half their faces. Oval, like the eyes of a praying mantis, they were pitch black and unblinking. Even worse than the eyes, though, was the absence of a mouth; the ghastly picture was rounded off with two pig-like snouts that dangled on either side of their cheeks. Eulalie gagged, grabbed her mouth and hunkered down further still.

'Did you hear something?' one asked and the full moon of a Pinpointer light reappeared, sliding through the giant's mouth.

'No I didn't. You're paranoid. Put down the search-light and help me tie this end. I can't do everything myself,' the obviously bossy one of the two replied, his voice shamelessly flaunting his irritation.

The light stopped right above Eulalie's head and then blinked out.

'I can't help it,' the whiny one replied, 'It's this thing on my face. It makes breathing difficult; and I hear things. My ears sing all the time. I'm gonna… take it off…'

'No! Don't,' Bossy shouted.

Eulalie crawled into the giant's cheek and satisfied with her cover, she pushed the curtain of shadows aside to spy on the men again. She was just in time to see one of them take off his face. Eulalie clasped her lips with both hands, just in case the ghastly noise that was trying to escape her lungs made it through.

'You idiot,' Bossy said. 'Now you'll have to go into quarantine when we get back. You know very well we're not supposed to breathe this air. You could be inhaling …bugs, poisonous spores or… bacteria or something.'

'I… I'm not scared.' Whiny pursed his lips and pushed out his chest, but he looked at his mask dangling in his hands as if he was having second thoughts. He rubbed under his nose. 'If these… things… that live here can breathe this air, so can I. I bet it's less polluted than ours anyway.' He then arched his back and took a deep, yawning breath, in the process turning to Eulalie, revealing to her great relief a very normal human looking face. Then, her relief slid into disappointment; they were not monsters, just men, cruel men.

What she had assumed to be double-pig-snouts, were in fact masks – that apparently protected them from the air. Eulalie sniffed. She couldn't find anything wrong with the air – rotten leaves, stale puddles, swamp rat droppings, a bit of smoke. Normal. And anyway, if you didn't smell like your surroundings by the end of an adventure, it hadn't been a successful one.

Whiny turned away from her again, picked up the end of the net and walked over to a nearby tree.

'Don't blame me if you get sick,' Bossy said and pulled another end of the net to a tree further away. 'You'll have to explain yourself. I won't give you an ounce of help. I *did* warn you.'

Disgusted, Eulalie watched the net take shape with each

new dangly end that was tied to a branch. It never seemed to end and could quite easily have covered a whole tree. It looked exactly like the spider web she had saved Rudolf from. No wonder none of the strands she had touched had been sticky - it hadn't been a creepy-crawly's craft after all. It was these Marauders. They were putting these nets up to catch the flying creatures. Eulalie scratched her head under her hat. These *men* were the monsters, setting traps to catch…uhm…monsters. Eulalie wished she could think of a politer word for the non-human monsters.

Almost forgetting that she was supposed to stay out of sight, she cleared her throat as a cloud of smoke slithered into the giant's mouth.

'Bless you,' Whiny said, thinking that it was Bossy who had sneezed.

'What? What you say?' Bossy asked.

'Nothing,' Whiny answered and sighed.

Eulalie hunkered down onto all fours and crawled to the giant's opposite cheek. She was still trying to figure out where they were keeping Rudolf. Hidden within the shadows again, her eyes swept the shrubs and low growth blanket of the tree-line.

Kahenna moved and shadows shifted. 'Rudolf… is… is that you?' she whispered.

Highlighted in a moonbeam of Kahenna's red as if in the spotlight of a stage, stood a hand-drawn cart that the Marauders must have pulled along with them. A multitude of rough cages were stacked, packed and squashed together on it. Eulalie could see dark shapes inside some of the cages. One was unmistakeable. Rudolf, the baby gargoyle sat curled up in the corner of the cage closest to her. His broken wing was draped on the floor of his prison like a loose mantle, while his unblinking eyes were clamped on Eulalie.

Holding onto the little one's stare, she sent him an encouraging smile and then slowly lowered herself out of sight again. Escape wasn't the priority anymore. This adventure had taken quite the turn. She had been expecting to save people from the monsters of the crimson night, but now she was planning on saving the monsters from people who had invaded their world their night.

FIFTEEN

LIKE WINDING UP A MUSIC BOX

'What should I do? What should I do?' Eulalie whispered. She stole a peek at the cart and hunkered down again. She desperately wanted to free the creatures from their cages, but it wouldn't help anyone or anything if she just went and got herself captured or even killed. She thumped her thighs as her heart's frustration battled her mind's logic.

Sometimes plans were too well hidden to be found and they had to reveal themselves. This was one of those moments. The plan knocked itself into her brain as she threw her back against the wall of the great stone cheek in exasperation – bashing her head against one of the giant's top back teeth in the process. As she rubbed the growing bump, Eulalie realised that she would wait for the Marauders to leave and then remove their nets. At least no other animals could be caught and injured like Rudolf then. That would also give her some time to search the deepest vestiges of her imagination and come up with a rescue plan that wasn't too patchy. Or, at least she'd have a bit of time to stitch the holes so that as little success as possible could drop out.

It didn't take the men long to have the net in place. Whiny looked around nervously. 'Come on then. Let's get this cart moving.'

'This place giving you the heebie-jeebies?' Bossy asked, his words peppered in mockery.

There was a kerfuffle of flapping wings, squawks and growls from the imprisoned animals. Eulalie dared peek between the knight's teeth.

The cart complained as the Marauders took a handle each and started pulling. Like a naughty child, it kicked in reluctant heels, leaving two clear furrows in the grass for anyone to follow.

'Relax, for goodness' sake,' Bossy said. 'You're beginning to make me twitchy.'

It tore at Eulalie's heart strings to watch little Rudolf go. She stole out from her hiding place, making sure that Rudolf saw her. His large eyes grew wider with every step as they moved further away from her. She didn't know whether he could understand her, but she kept on mouthing, 'I'm coming for you, I'm coming for you.' He clasped the bars of his prison with his tiny hands, refusing to let go of Eulalie's gaze until the shadows severed the connection.

*

Cli-creak, cli-creak, cli-creak, the Marauder's cart limped over the uneven ground, moaning with every half-revolution of its two wheels. After Eulalie had successfully removed the nets from the trees, she didn't even need to follow the tracks to find the cart. With the grating planks arguing with the rusty axle about the sharpness of the high notes, she easily located them and could even quite happily stomp on behind in no fear of being heard.

Whiny kept looking back, though. Once or twice he nearly caught her exposed and out in the open, but her quick reflexes and the confusing shadows cast by Kahenna's red light had rendered her mostly invisible.

'Stop looking back all the time,' Bossy complained when Whiny was mid-turn.

'But I think we're being followed,' Whiny replied, feeling quite dejected.

'I've told you a hundred times that it's just the shadows. Nothing would dare follow us,' Bossy boasted.

'But…but what if there *is* something there?' Whiny asked, eyes wide, 'This world is *full* of creepy things.'

'Oh for crying out loud,' Bossy abraded and let go of his cart handle. The weight made Whiny stumble forwards.

'Hey. At least warn me next time before you …' Whiny's words were interrupted by the tower of cages swaying. He flung his arms around them to prevent imminent disaster. The topmost planked-prison slipped straight into his forehead, bumping the promise of a bruise above his brow. Whatever was imprisoned inside it hissed and spat at the face plastered to the crooked window bars.

'Ouch,' Whiny recoiled and cupped his hands to the bump on his head, 'That hurt.'

'Don't you ever stop moaning?' Bossy asked. 'You know what?' Bossy rubbed his mask-chin and faced Whiny. 'If you and I had been at school together, I would have made your life Hell. You're a weakling, like Snotty, Four-Eyes, Lanky and Cry-Baby…' he smirked at some memory that gave him obvious pleasure, 'You would have fit in perfectly with that group. It's a pity you weren't there…to help share their bruises.'

An uninvited shiver clasped Eulalie's lower back and clambered up to her neck. That's exactly what her brother was like; always trying to ruin her happiness because he couldn't find his own. He was obviously not alone in this world. There were more like him; more who treated others as punch bags.

As if Bossy could hear her thoughts, he turned his gaze on the reed bush that was doubling as Eulalie's cover. She held her breath and bit her lip.

'Give me a Wind-Up,' Bossy said and held out his hand.

'We don't have all night. Come on.' His fingers flicked irritably.

Whiny fumbled with one of his leather pouches and had it open in no time. Swiftly, he removed something about the size of a large potato and handed it to Bossy.

A Wind-Up? What's a Wind-Up? Eulalie thought. She squinted to try and see what he held. From where she was hiding it almost looked like a huge glittery beetle – like the ones that rolled balls of poop around, but much larger.

Bossy snatched it from Whiny and inspected it. 'Yes,' he said. 'At least you've kept these clean.' He lobbed it back to Whiny, who had to juggle it to prevent it from slipping through his fingers.

'You wind it up. I'll shoot. With your aim I might end up with a crossbow bolt in my rear end,' Bossy said while unslinging what looked like an arm-length piece of wood with a bow attached to the end. Pushing one end against his stomach, he pulled the string and it clicked into place. Moments later, he had one of those short arrows resting on the wood.

That's what they'd been using. That's what put the hole in my hat – and the holes in Lancaster Gate, Eulalie thought with a gulp.

'Do it,' Bossy hissed, sliding the weapon to his shoulder.

Eulalie didn't know what was about to happen. She lowered herself again, making sure that she could still see part of what the Marauders were up to, just in case she had to sacrifice her cover in order to flee.

A loud creaking noise flowed out of the Wind-up. Whiny's hand was moving as if he was turning a key. It reminded her of the music box she and momma had once seen in a shop. The creaking slowed down and completely ceased. 'She's ready,' he said failing to hide the eagerness in his voice.

'Good,' Bossy replied. 'Now remember to keep your eyes open – but stand dead still. It's programmed to pick up *any* movement.' He bent his knees slightly and lowered his head in readiness.

'Now,' Bossy ordered him.

Whiny threw his hands up as if releasing a captured twinkling star. The Wind-up whirred, stuttered and flew up into the air.

The shiny object hovered as if uncertain at first, before finding its rhythm. It shot up into the night and started hovering at about half-a tree's height. Eulalie couldn't blink, just in case she missed what it was doing. The Wind-up was grotesque and beautiful at the same time. Lights started blinking on its body as it swayed from side to side and hovered like a kestrel.

Five, six, seven thin lines of light then burst from its silver body. Like spider webs struggling to find a hold, the lights bounced around drunkenly, to leaves, to shrubs, to stumps, to trunks, until they fused together in a shaky, thick line that connected to Whiny's stomach.

'I said stand still,' Bossy said through ground teeth.

'I am,' Whiny replied.

'Then stop blinking. Stop breathing if you have to…don't even think,' Bossy said.

That appeared to help. The line of light was severed and the buzzing silver insect swayed and shivered further along. Every so often a burst of thin lines erupted from its body and connected to the swamp below it. The lights danced and pirouetted around in their search for movement. It was slowly making its way towards

Eulalie. She could hear the whirring of its metal wings begin to slow down.

Closer and closer it flew, until it came to a terrifying halt right above the reed bush where she was hiding. Now that it was so close to her, Eulalie heard something click in the strange mechanism. Moments later lines of light rained from its glinting body again. They scoured the gently swaying reeds, the unwelcome, unnatural light making shadows quiver and dance. One or two of the needles of light found Eulalie and ran over her knees. More bright filaments traced the contours of the veins on the back of her hand. The Wind-up's wings slowed. The tiny spotlights moved to her face, her cheeks, her nose…

'It's found something…shoot,' Whiny shouted.

Eulalie kicked her leg back and a bunch of reeds whiplashed and waved their thin arms. Instantly the lights released their sticky grips from Eulalie and fused together, highlighting the un-opened seed pod of a tall reed.

Thwack! The crossbow sneezed and spat out the bolt. A loud whistle rushed towards Eulalie and half a heartbeat later she felt her boot shudder, the force pushing her foot at a nasty angle. She nearly screamed, but the jolt in her leg was instantly followed by something heavy and metallic dropping onto her head. She swallowed her scream in a hiccup and dived under her arms for cover.

The windup lay right next to her elbow.

Eulalie looked at the strange contraption. It did, indeed look like a bug, but it had no head. Instead, it had a ring of eyes – most probably the lights, all around its body. Its wings were strange too. There were five of them mounted on the metal insect's sides, but they didn't look much like the wings of an insect; more like the sails of her mill – only tiny. One of them still whirred in a fast circle, and then it, too, stopped. Right in the centre of its back it carried a winding screw – Eulalie had been correct; it was indeed like the music box. She picked it up, pinching it between her thumb and forefinger.

'Aargh, waste of time,' came Bossy's voice. 'You didn't wind it up tight enough. And there's nothing there anyway. Most probably just the wind. Go fetch the Wind-up.'

'W…why me? It's dark there. What if it was a snake or something poisonous?' Whiny asked.

'Just go fetch it, stupid. Stop complaining and do what you're told. Take the lantern if you're such a coward,' Bossy said.

Eulalie had nowhere to go. Bossy had his weapon ready. She pulled her legs up in readiness to run, but her boot snagged on the other. 'Blessed Moons,' she whispered. 'My boot.' The arrow had completely pierced her boot. 'Nearly took my toes off. It's a good thing my feet are so small.'

A light approached. The reeds' shadows swayed and waved, urging Eulalie to get away. Like a will-o'-the-wisp, the lights danced and rocked as Whiny came closer.

Without thinking, Eulalie rolled the Wind-up away from her. It landed with a thud not far from her hiding place. Then she rolled herself into a tight ball, like a hedgehog would when threatened.

'Found it,' she heard Whiny call out. He was so close, it almost sounded as if he was speaking to her. His hurried footsteps thumped and splashed almost in time with her heart. The light faded, the shadows stopped shivering. It was only when the *cli-*

creak, cli-creak, cli-creak song started again, that Eulalie dared remove her hands from her head.

Wet, half covered in mud, bruised and scratched Eulalie sat up and looked at her boot. She reached her hand towards the feathered tail sticking out one side and razor tip the other. Then, she balled her hands into tight fists and cradled her fingers to her heart – her hands were cold, that must be why they were shaking so much.

SIXTEEN
RAVENSCOURT PARK

'You're not helping,' Eulalie whispered and looked at Kahenna. The crimson moon didn't appear to have moved across the sky at all, but sideways along with her as if she, too, was wanting to be a part of this adventure. Watching the moon peek at her through the trees, Eulalie thought that it was no wonder that so many people got lost in her light. Like two happy children, the moon and time appeared to be holding hands, skipping together on the horizon in no particular direction.

Eulalie angled the *London Underground Mind the Gap Map* to borrow some of Kahenna's light; her fingers slid over the small page along the line she assumed they had travelled. 'Ravenscourt Park,' Eulalie said to the moon. She shuffled along the branch of the swamp oak tree and kneeled down to get a better look. A raven cawed – it sounded as if he needed to clear his throat. Eulalie cleared hers. Moments later a chorus of ravens burst into murderous laughter. Whatever the first raven had said, the others had found it deadly funny. 'Definitely.' She inspected the back of her hands – they had stopped shaking, but she hated seeing her freckled skin without Spookasem's dot.

'I did *not* invite you,' she whispered when a tear slid down her cheek. She swatted it away as if it was an annoying fly.

Ignoring the pang in her heart, she squinted at her surroundings. She had been here before – many times, but never on a Crimson Night. And without her thin blue chord, she felt severed from the tavern. She looked back at her map again.

Whoever made the map must also have had their bearings wrong because it wasn't nearly to scale – and many of the place names, like Kensington Olympia, Gloucester Road and West Kensington didn't make sense at all. There weren't any particular trees, rocky mounds, ruins or landmarks of any sort that could help her associate the areas with the names. Sighing, she looked up at the stars through the canopy of the tree and found the shy star with whom she always shared wishes. 'Do I have it wrong after all? If you could talk, would you share the secret of this map with me? You know all *my* secrets. Is the answer to this map up there? With you?' The star blinked but didn't answer.

Eulalie put the map away. Then she clambered higher into the tree.

Whiny and Bossy had left the cart just outside the boundary of trees that framed the clearing of Ravenscourt. Oak, Alder, Wishing-Willow, Aspen and Man-Groves leaned like injured sentries against each other. The old were holding up the young, the young were supporting the old. All were beaten and broken by their long war with snow, wind and relentless rain. Ravens, magpies, crows and jackdaws favoured that eerie area; holding court, settling old skirmishes with the odd bare-feather-flutter but mostly just gossiping. One of the adventures on Eulalie and Spookasem's *to-do-lists* – and there were many – was to raise a raven chick, teach it to speak and then ask it what the gossiping was all about. Working out how to hide a talking raven from her dadda was a large problem, though, so *that* adventure had been on hold for quite some time.

Eulalie craned her neck. A number of lights were shining through the trees and every so often harsh laughter, a cough or the odd sneeze would poison the night. Eulalie simply had to get closer.

*

'Why always me?' Whiny asked. He rolled his eyes and his shoulders sagged. With a groan he hoisted one of the cages off the cart. Straining his back, he limped with the burden back into the clearing. Three boxes remained; the one that imprisoned little Rudolf, however was nowhere to be seen. She would rescue all she could, though.

'This is it,' Eulalie whispered to herself and stole a couple of steps towards the cart, but footsteps and muttering made her swirl around. She flattened herself behind a large swamp-termite mound. She hoped that the tiny bugs with their stinging pincers were sleeping. Cold and wet seeped through the new hole in her boot.

'Clarence do this, and Clarence do that, and Clarence why'd you take your mask off and Clarence, you'll never come here with us again. I should *never* have come to this god-forsaken world in the first place,' Whiny said as he emerged from the shadows.

Whiny. So, his name is actually Clarence, Eulalie thought. She had become so used to the name Whiny, that Clarence didn't appear to suit him at all. *But what was he talking about? Another world? Maybe he meant another city.*

Clarence walked to the cart, but instead of lifting another one of the crates, he fumbled in his pocket and lifted something out.

Eulalie's heart gave a jolt as it occurred to her that it might be another one of the Wind-ups. She willed her body to become flatter as she pushed herself against the mound of ant sand-castle – *hey, perhaps this is Elephant Ant Castle,* she thought, making a mental note to check her map. *Or maybe one of the other termite mounds somewhere in the swamp… wait a moment, could that mean that there are elephants in the swamp too? Or maybe just a mound the size of an elephant.*

Eulalie peered around the mound and then her heart gave another jolt. Whiny…or rather Clarence had Spookasem. That was what he was holding. It was Spookasem's ink well.

Clarence lifted the tiny bottle up to the light and shook it. 'Strange glass; looks old. Anyway, let's see what's inside,' he said and pinched the cork stopper to pull it out. For a moment Eulalie became excited – maybe Spookasem would appear. But what would happen if only *she* could call him up? Clarence would only be wasting the ink then.

'Clarence, what's taking you so long?' someone asked.

Eulalie didn't recognise this voice. It was most certainly too high to belong to Bossy.

Someone emerged from the trees, shadows pulling apart like stage curtains opening for an actor. 'What's that you got?' Even though smaller than Clarence, the newcomer seemed to assert some sort of authority over him.

'What's it to you? My business,' Clarence said, tossing the bottle of ink into the air and snatching it right in front of the masked face, before dropping it into his pocket.

Poor Spookasem, Eulalie thought. *I hope he doesn't puke in the bottle.* Eulalie grimaced at the thought.

'What do you want?' Clarence put on his best assertive voice and leaned against the cart.

Those large, round mask eyes stared lifeless at him. 'No need to be rude. I just came to say hello. I'm Adelaide. I was new once too. You'll get used to things out here. This world's not *that* bad. Just as long as you follow the rules and stay away from whatever is at the top of the food chain. I've got a theory that if there *was* a way of entering this place when the red moon was *not* out, it might actually be liveable.' She traced a teasing finger over one of the boxes on the back of the cart. 'Anyway, Leroy wants these boxes…those *things* inside.' Her shoulders gave an over-exaggerated shiver. 'You just need to stop messing up,' Adelaide said. Eulalie could hear her smile.

'Bah, Leroy. I'm not afraid of him,' Clarence said. 'And anyway, I *hate* this world. Why would *anyone* want to live here; even on non-red days? It'd bore me to death. It's primitive. No technology. The natives do everything by horse, cart and other animals that poop and stink.'

Leroy - that must be Bossy's real name, Eulalie thought. She frowned as she tried to put the puzzle of the rest of his words together.

'*Our* world doesn't have *magic*,' Adelaide said. She stretched the words *our* and *magic*, making her fantastical statement sound all too real.

Eulalie's ear pricked up. Did Adelaide mean that there was, in fact, magic here? Eulalie, of course, never doubted its existence, but it was good to hear it confirmed by others too.

'Anyway, Leroy wants you to remove the wings of those things you and he caught,' Adelaide said.

What? Eulalie thought that she must have heard wrong. *Remove the wings? No.*

Clarence and Adelaide looked in her direction as if they could hear her panicking heart.

'Mighty creepy out there,' Clarence finally said. 'That feeling that there's always something watching you never ceases.'

'You're paranoid. I bet you'd shoot your own shadow if you had a loaded weapon in your hands. Anyway, Leroy says he wants all this business wrapped up before *M* returns,' Adelaide said.

'Who's *M*?' Clarence asked. He was trying to sound tough, but his voice betrayed him; his words were thin and sticky like the skin on steaming milk.

Who's M? Eulalie thought. She couldn't recall hearing any mention of *M* so far.

'So you haven't met him yet?' Adelaide asked. There was a warning embedded somewhere in those words. 'Can't ever mention his name in public. Doesn't want to be associated with the likes of us. Don't worry, you'll meet him sometime. Just make sure you remove those wings before he comes.'

'Why me?' Clarence was beginning to feel the roots of panic take hold. He didn't like the threats about this *M* person.

'The new guy always gets to do the dirty stuff,' Adelaide said. Without assisting Clarence with the box lifting, she turned and walked away. 'I still can't believe you removed your mask. *M definitely* won't be happy about *that*,' she said as if talking to herself. There was a *rather-you-than-me* enjoyment that clung to the air where she had stood.

'Cursed, cursed place,' Clarence moaned under his breath. 'I can't believe you removed your mask,' he repeated her words in his best, mock-Adelaide voice. Then, he rolled his shoulder as if in pain, un-latched the buckle of one of his shoulder belts and flung it onto the ground. 'I hate this cursed place.' He kicked the belt. 'No matter how much they pay me, I'll never return.'

Then, to Eulalie's dismay, he stacked the last three boxes

on top of each other. Cursing and moaning, he hoisted them up and stumbled drunkenly into Ravenscourt Park, leaving nothing for her to save.

'What now?' Eulalie asked. Her heart raced, overtaking her desperate thoughts and kicking dust into her panicked eyes. She took two steps towards the nearest tree, but then turned and hid behind the termite kingdom again.

Think. Think. Ignoring the bulging bruise on her head, she knocked her fist into her forehead, hoping some inspiration would be shaken loose.

Something must have happened, because an idea stuck her – quite hard too.

Eulalie's eyes flicked to the shoulder belt still lying in the mud, then at Clarence's mask, and finally the termite mound.

It was crazy, it was desperate, but she had to do something – and quick.

One last time Eulalie looked around, her gaze stepping into every shadow. It was one of those forsaken, lonely moments where she searched for someone; anyone who might be able to help her, but the shadows revealed none.

In the distance, someone laughed.

A raven cawed.

Eulalie decided there was no point looking around for a hero - and made up her mind to become one herself – and then tell Spookasem all about it later.

SEVENTEEN
HOLDING OR CHOPPING?

'Maybe if I…' Clarence's voice whined.

'Finally,' Eulalie whispered. She had nearly missed him and gone right past. Trying to act as casual as possible - confident to make it look as though she belonged, but not arrogant enough to attract unnecessary attention - she marched around the back of the large tent and straight through the entrance.

A quick glance across the clearing had revealed two masked figures sitting by a fire, but they hadn't even looked up from whatever had been keeping them busy. The tent flap closed behind her.

'Maybe I should…' Clarence was standing behind a dirty looking table; indecision written all over his uncertain movements. One hand was fumbling with a dangerous-looking meat cleaver, his fingers not quite sure what to do with it. The other was pinning a bird on a table. One of its little wings, feathers bedraggled, was pinched between the Marauder's fingers. Eulalie didn't know what she would've done if there had been another Marauder in the tent.

Clarence bit his lip. He breathed in the last of the courage that hadn't leaked out of him yet. Then, with a resigned sigh, he raised the cleaver above his head and pinched his eyes shut.

As if anticipating their fate, the boxes and cages all over the room exploded into a dangerous silence. The creatures imprisoned within the rusty bars pulled into tight corners, urging the shadows to render them invisible from the imminent harm.

'Clarence…' Eulalie said. She froze at his name. She had forgotten what she had planned to say. Her eyes tried to hold his hand up – prevent him from bringing the weapon down on the bird's wing – or his own hand, as his eyes were still shut. Eulalie's heart was trying to thump-start her lungs breathing again.

Clarence halted with the cleaver loaded high above his head. His hand was shaking so much that he was in imminent danger of dropping it onto his own head – or worse, the little bird. He sneaked a peak through an eye-lid. The momentary distraction pulled lines of relief over his face. He had forgotten to try and look mean.

Both he and Eulalie breathed out when he lowered the clever.

He looked at Eulalie, waiting. The bird's legs kicked.

'What *now*?' he asked. 'You can tell Leroy that I'm doing what he's asked me to.' Then he frowned and Eulalie could see his eyes move from her masked face, up and down her clothing and then back to her face where his gaze searched for her eyes; she was glad that they were hidden.

Eulalie knew that her disguise wasn't very convincing. Veiled in *his* mask and with *his* pouched belt wrapped from her shoulder to hip, half-concealing her own, she was hoping that the shadows and mastery of distraction would hide the rest of her from him.

'Uhm, I've just arrived,' she stumbled. Her heart sounded like a horse galloping in a drum with the mask pulled over most of her face. With her breathing so unnaturally high, her goggled eyes were fogging up. Eulalie tried to hold her breath, but that only made her heart beat faster.

'So?' Clarence asked. He looked doubtful… nervous… jumpy. Eulalie had to put him at ease.

'I've just … I'm new, so Leroy said I needed to come and help you. He said that the new ones like us always do the dirty jobs,' she said and bit her lip.

'Yip, that's Leroy for you. Most probably thinks I'm useless, so he sends me some *help*,' Clarence said.

Eulalie didn't respond. It sounded as if he was talking to himself.

'Your clothes look funny. Where you from?' he asked.

'The…that's what we wear…at the coast. I'm from the coast,' Eulalie answered. She wished that she had had more time to plan some answers.

'Which one?' he asked, rolling the clever in his fingers.

'Which one?' Eulalie asked.

'Yes, stupid. Which coast? East or west?' Still sounding rude, Clarence did however appear to be losing some of his initial suspicion.

'The…the…west. I'm from the west coast,' Eulalie said. She bit her lip again. *Please, please believe me. I'm not lying.*

'What's your name?' Clarence asked. His shoulders relaxed.

A wave of relief washed over Eulalie. Asking for names – last part of acceptance.   'Eu…Eu…Madigan.' Eulalie nearly gave her name away. *Madigan* was her momma's last name.

'Eumadigan? Sounds strange. I've never heard *that* one before. Must be a west coast thing,' he said. The cleaver dropped onto the chopping board with a metallic *thunk*.

'It's actually just Madigan,' Eulalie said. She felt the warm glow of colour flowing back into her cheeks.

'Still sounds funny to me,' he said. 'Anyway, *Just* Madigan from the west coast – which would you prefer? Holding or chopping?' Clarence asked.

'…what…?'

Clarence rolled his eyes. 'Leroy surely *did* send me a stupid one. 'Holding…?' He lifted his hand still gripping the poor bird. 'Or chopping…?' He picked up the cleaver and waved it about.

'I… uhm… chop… no, holding.' Eulalie was desperate to get the bird out of his clutches.

'Huh, thought so. Easy option. Well, don't just stand there, come and hold the creature. We've got a long night ahead of us,' he said.

When he shoved the bird into her hands, Eulalie saw his eyes flick to her stained fingers. He squinted and then searched for her eyes again. Eulalie didn't know whether the fluttering she felt in her hands was the bird's heart or her own.

'Now, spread the wing with one hand. Whoa! Don't let the thing get away.' Clarence pushed on her hand to make her fingers clasp tighter onto the bird, exactly what Eulalie was trying to avoid. She didn't want to scare it any further. 'Push it onto the table and don't move; unless you want me to get rid of those … those stained fingers of yours.'

Eulalie had to act quickly. She held the little bird against the table-top. Clarence stared at it and slowly lifted the cleaver. Her free hand strayed and unclasped one, two, three of the buckled pouches she was wearing. She grimaced and prepared herself for pain – and lots of it. At least she was expecting it. Clarence wouldn't be, so it would hurt him far, far worse. He wouldn't hesitate forever. It was now or never.

EIGHTEEN
HAND IN FLAMES

Flinching and biting down onto her lip, Eulalie stuck her hand into the pouch; it might as well have been into fire. Almost instantly, her hand burst into invisible flames as the termites she had coaxed into the pouches found her skin. Tears streamed down her face and welled up in the corners where the mask pressed into her skin. She flicked her hand in Clarence's direction, hoping that some of the termites would find him just as delicious.

By the time she stuck her hand into the second pouch, the burn had turned into a red-hot cold. It was one of those pains that tasted of metal and bitter-screams in the mouth. Once again, she flicked her hand towards him. *Come on, come on.*

A swollen, itchy numbness blanketed her fingers by the time she found the third pouch. This time she rubbed her hand onto his shoulder.

'Hey, watcha doin…? The rest of his words caught fire. Clarence didn't even try and put the cleaver down gently. It dropped as he slapped his neck. Eulalie swung to him. She saw the scream on his lips and she clamped her termite-covered hand over his mouth, keeping the bird well away from him.

Bitter prints of inexpressible pain welled up in his eyes as a trail of termites migrated from her hand to his face.

'Don't scream,' she hissed.

He slapped his neck, then scraped his fingernails into his hair. A strange humming noise was beginning to boil at the back of his throat.

'Leroy will think you're a wuss.' Eulalie hoped that he knew what it meant to be a wuss. Her brother called her that all the time.

Clarence's eyes bulged and he blinked an ocean of tears.

Eulalie gripped his arm and escorted him to the flap of the tent. 'Go, I'll do the wings,' she said. 'Sneak around the corner and wash it off with fresh poop. Buffalo poop works best. Go. Quick.'

Clarence nodded and Eulalie removed her hand from his quivering mouth.

He slapped his neck on the other side, then the back of his arm, then the top of his head.

'Go. I've got your back. Go.' If Eulalie herself hadn't been so close to tears, she would have laughed.

Clarence actually thanked her when he ran. Well, at least it sounded like a very mumbled 'thanks,' that toiled with a suppressed scream behind his gritted teeth.

Lifting her mask, so as not to scare the little bird any more, she whispered, 'now stay away from webs, little one.' Then, stretching as far as possible out of the flap without drawing too much attention to her movement, she tossed the bird into the air. The night welcomed it back with a starry embrace.

Eulalie rolled back into the tent and half cart-wheeled out of the belt around her shoulder. There followed some slapping, rubbing, itching and some more slapping before she could continue her rescue efforts.

Satisfied that most of her feisty travelling companions had been encouraged to go and bite something else, Eulalie looked at the boxes and cages. She had drawn quite the shady crowd. Shadows of all shapes and degrees of elongation stared at her with large glowing eyes, unblinking slanted eyes, drifting firefly eyes and cat-like broken-glass eyes. And one pair of eyes were the night-sky-deep walnut eyes of the baby gargoyle. He had shrugged off his shadows and was almost clothed in the stick-like bars of his prison as he pressed towards his potential freedom.

'Rudolf,' Eulalie said and smiled a first-taste-of-a-honeycomb-smile.

The little gargoyle must also have stolen some honey from a hive before, because it smiled exactly the same way back at Eulalie.

*

The large-scale rescue began without incident. Rudolf had clambered all over Eulalie, lick-kissing every part of her exposed face as she had rushed around unlatching boxes. The two of them watched a peculiar coiled shadow slither its way through the open door of its box, revealing itself to being a snake. By the time the snake had revealed its avian properties and become airborne, the tent had turned into a carnival.

Pointy shoes tapped, large ears flapped, wing-like capes fluttered over hidden faces and coiled hats flopped over eyes. There was low flying, high hovering, hissing and bell-like chuckles and together, it all turned into one kaleidoscope of chaos. In the end, Eulalie stopped trying to decipher where shadows joined feet and where swooping belonged to the shadows. *Anything* that moved had the potential of being trampled on, or trampling her, so Eulalie avoided *everything* that moved with near impossible acrobatic manoeuvres.

The most impressive of all the feats, however, had been the fact that this frenzied parade to freedom had taken place in almost perfect silence.

Standing in boots of sweat, Eulalie admired the scene of the rescue. She had to squint to see past the veil of dust that curtained the end of the show. Flickering for a flaming encore, the candles around the room were giving it their best, while shadows stretched to catch a last glimpse of the performers as they made their exits.

Just as impressed by the quality of the show, Rudolf, who was sat on Eulalie's shoulder, tail coiled around her neck, squeaked as if asking, *is it over?*

'Did you see the snake leave?' Eulalie asked Rudolf. Her shoulders were heaving with every breath. 'I haven't seen him since *that* box…no, *that* one ended up *there*.' Eulalie pointed at a box stacked on another at an angle that shouldn't have been possible. 'Maybe it's …Spookasem!'

Eulalie dashed forwards and collapsed in the middle of the tent, where the inkwell lay hidden in the protective embrace of an upturned table. In a flash, the stopper was open. Smiling from ear to ear-less, she pushed the inky cork to the back of her hand, adding another freckle to her natural selection.

NINETEEN
THE RETURN OF THE INKLING

'Zap. Zap. Take that. And… that. Expel. Dispel. Propel,' Spookasem said. He appeared in an explosion of ghostly clouds. With a theatrical flourish, he swung his wide-sleeved robes as if he were a fluttering peacock. His mouth was pulled in lines of seriousness as he spat out words of power. The shroud of dust he was pirouetting in danced and coiled in gossamer threads with his every movement.

'Spook…' Eulalie ducked just in time as his weapon – a grotesque stick about the length of his forearm, made its dangerous arc over Eulalie's head, barely missing Rudolf.

'Spook. Shhhh. There are …' She ducked a second time when his arm circled back.

The Inkling swung around and pointed the stick at her. 'Don't move a muscle, fiend. This wand is loaded and I'm not afraid to use it.' Then recognition dawned on him in flashing blinks. 'Eulalie? Rudolf? Get down. We're in the middle of a war.'

'Spookasem. Keep your voice low, or you'll start one,' Eulalie said as he pushed her down, his too-large robes covering her like a wet vulture's wings. Rudolf thought the game of earlier was starting again. He smiled.

'What are you doing here?' Spookasem whispered.

'I'm on a rescue mission. What in the name of the four moons are *you* doing?' Eulalie asked.

The Inkling looked around, not recognising his surroundings at all. 'Oh. I see,' he said.

'Spook. Tell me *now*. What's going on?' Eulalie demanded.

'Uhm,' he cleared his throat and said, 'I was in the middle of this wand battle in a school. It was crazy. Battle to the death. Us inside, them outside. I was flinging spells left right and centre.' He closed one eye and peered tentatively into the tip of his wand. 'Expel?' he asked and flinched. 'Dud. Must've run out. Anyway. What you doing? Hey Rudolf…'

'Keep your voice down,' Eulalie pleaded. 'We're literally in the middle of a Marauder camp. I've just set all the creatures free; well I think they're all free. I can't find the snake…'

'Setting the creatures free? Who are you talking to?' Bully, or rather, Leroy asked. His voice intruded into Eulalie's post mortem of the mission.

Rudolf hissed.

Eulalie and Spookasem whirled around to face the flap of the tent. Barring their only escape, were Leroy and Clarence. Leroy's face was still hidden behind his mask, while Clarence's face was smeared in what appeared to be a wet, muddy, dripping mask.

Spookasem sniffed the air and said, 'Buffalo poop. Nice. So, are you going to introduce me to your smelly friends?'

'Clarence,' Leroy said. His hiss dripped with an unseen venom. 'Explain to me how a strange creature ended up in this tent, setting all our captive animals free while you were playing in the swamp, rolling around in buffalo poop?'

'I… uhm …thought that she was …she had a mask on and I couldn't …termites bit me and I had to …Eumadigan…no, just Madigan…buffalo poop…made me feel better…' No matter what angle Clarence approached the story from, he always appeared the fool.

Spookasem still didn't appear to realise what danger Eulalie was in. He was swaying his wand around, whispering strange incantations as though he expected something to happen. Every failed attempt at whatever spell he was trying to cast, he would peer down the tip of the stick.

'A few heartbeats ago I was shaking the foundations of buildings with this thing; and now it seems... uhm...Eulalie, maybe you try,' Spookasem said, holding the stick out to her.

'Spook. These are the people who tried to kill us earlier.' Eulalie spoke through the side of pursed lips, hoping that Leroy and Clarence wouldn't notice. Rudolf's little body was shaking so much that Eulalie lifted him down from her shoulders and hugged him into her chest.

Leroy finally released Eulalie from his stare as he looked around the room. 'What manner of creature are you? Either you are barking mad, or there is someone else in here,' he said, taking a step into the tent. Clarence followed.

When he couldn't see anyone else, Leroy turned back to Eulalie. Icy fingers of terror gripped her neck and the back of her head, guiding her face to the weapon that was slung over Leroy's shoulders. He followed her eyes.

'My crossbow? Great weapon, isn't it?' Leroy asked. Faster than a heartbeat, he hoisted it over his shoulder, pointing the tip of the bolt straight at Eulalie's heart.

'Eulalie,' Spookasem gasped. He stretched his arms and stepped in front of her.

'You haven't answered my question, young lady. What manner of creature are you? Why set our beasts free?' Leroy asked. His voice carried a low chill into the tent.

'They're not yours,' Eulalie said. She shoved Spookasem out of the way. She wanted to face up to this bully. 'They don't belong to you. I saw the nets you were setting. I heard that you wanted to chop their wings off.'

Eulalie was pleased that the fear that she had felt earlier had been smoothed over by the heat of an early flame that would soon burn to anger. There wasn't a trace of terror in her voice.

'Leroy…' Clarence hissed into Leroy's ear. 'Don't get too close to her. Look at her face. I think she's diseased.'

'Remove your hat,' Leroy said. He was still pointing the crossbow at her, but he had moved his head in order to see her better.

Eulalie's eyes flicked to the tent-flap.

'Child. There is nowhere for you to go… except the afterlife. You won't get two steps towards this exit. Now, remove your hat,' Leroy said.

Eulalie pursed her lips.

'Oh dear,' Spookasem said. 'I know that look.'

Eulalie ignored him and slowly lifted her hat. Like a sea anemone opening up, the top of her head exploded in a ferocious forest of brilliant red. The shadows that had stretched over her face ran for cover, revealing a face that mirrored the constellations above and mapped out frozen lakes and rivers.

Leroy shuddered and stepped back, stumbling into Clarence, who failed to swallow a high pitched *eek*. One arm still aimed the crossbow at Eulalie's heart, the other pushed the mask tighter onto his face.

'Clarence, see I told you not to take off your mask,' Leroy said. He shuffled back. 'What *are* you?' he asked. 'I won't ask again. What are you?' Leroy's finger was curled around a release trigger. It creaked in anticipation.

Eulalie didn't know what to say, so she stated the obvious. 'I…I'm a girl.'

'Then… then *what* manner of disease do you carry on your …?'

'Leroy. Leroy!' Adelaide burst into the tent and crashed full-speed into Clarence. Their entangled bodies, in turn, collided with Leroy.

'Adelaide, you idiotic imbecilic fool. Get off m…' Leroy shouted, kicking and wriggling to undo the knot of arms, legs and curses.

'That. That monster she's holding. There's another outside, but huge,' Adelaide cried.

TWENTY
MURDERER OF STONE

Something heavy dropped onto the tent. A large bulge bent half the roof inwards. Eulalie and Spookasem dived for cover; everyone else ducked. Not built for carrying such weight, the thick canvas walls of the tent leaned and the poles bent and groaned like wind-swept trees.

A dangerous snap and ping cut through the air. Eulalie screamed, thinking that Leroy had shot the bolt at her. But another followed and another and another.

'The tent pegs, the tent's gonna fall...' Clarence was interrupted by a final violent *snap – snap – snap,* as tent ropes ripped apart and a high-pitched whistle when something small and very fast was catapulted into the night with the releasing rope.

Moments later, the whole tent – and mother gargoyle – collapsed onto them.

'Eulalie, this way,' Spook managed to grab hold of Eulalie's wrist and placed her hand on the back of his heel.

'Go, Spook, go. I'll hold on.' With Rudolf cradled in her arm, shielded from the crushing canvas, she leaned onto her Inkling's leg as he crawled to what she hoped was a way out of the sea of fabric. Somewhere behind her, she could hear a melting pot of curses and panicked voices as Leroy, Clarence and Adelaide were also battling to free themselves from the claustrophobic mess.

'Fire, fire!'

'The canvas caught fire.'

Between all the swearing, those words were the only ones that mattered. They needed to get out fast.

'I ...think ...' *Plonk.* 'Ouch. That was my head. This way...?' Spookasem cursed. He had no idea which way he was going.

'Spook, you need to hurry. I can smell the smoke,' Eulalie cried.

From outside the scene was quite the comical one. The canvas bulged and flapped like the sea in a tempest. Stormy shouts and thunderous curses rumbled from beneath the roiling fabric waves as Leroy fought not to drown in the palaver. Swimming around blindly in an ocean of panic, Adelaide snapped her teeth at anything that came too close to her; unfortunately Clarence did. He thrashed wildly when teeth clamped into his shin – and the harder he fought to get away from the canvas shark, the tighter she held on.

Close to them, a flame was indeed trying to take hold. If it had been a dog, you could have said it was more bark than bite. The fire choked on the damp canvas, coughing up more smoke than it spat flame.

Eulalie rolled free from the edge of the canvas into Kahenna's light. She saw the Inkling's hand emerge looking like a spluttering spider where it tapped the ground. 'Spookasem. Here. Take my hand.' She locked fingers with the Inkling. He kicked wildly as she tore him free of the roiling mass.

Arms flung over each other's shoulders, the two bundles of bruises hurried off and were swallowed by the trees.

'Eulalie, when did the rules of this game change?' Spookasem asked.

'It's not a game anymore, Spook, it's not a game anymore,' Eulalie answered. Leaving behind the burden of any doubt, Eulalie's voice was cut-glass and crystal clear.

Just as the fire breathed its last, Leroy managed to find an edge of the fabric and force himself free. He was closely followed by Adelaide, who had lost her mask in the process and Clarence, who *was* now wearing one.

'Go. Go. Go! Get every last one of those Wind-ups, now. I want all of those contraptions in the air yesterday.'

Even though Leroy was shouting orders at the top of his voice, Eulalie didn't manage to hear all of them. What she did hear was 'Wind-ups.' That was all she needed to hear to ignore the ache in her legs and run faster. Never in her wildest dreams did she imagine that an adventure that started with kidnapping poultry, would lead to her fearing for her life.

*

'Spook,' Eulalie screamed. She halted within the burnt embers and ashes of her hope and joy. A grey blanket of despair dropped over her. 'Spook. Spook. Spook. Help. Take him.' She turned around so suddenly, Spookasem barely managed to come to a halt with a muddy slide.

'What? What? Now's not the time to sto…'

Every part of Eulalie's small frame shuddered as the last supports of her being cracked, crumbled and tumbled down. Her face soured into a first-taste-of-a-lemon, before she burst out crying and crumbled to her knees.

'I'm a murderer…' She hiccupped and gasped at the air that her tears had stolen from her. All manners of liquids seeped out of her eyes, nose and mouth, turning her face into a speckled beach in a storm surge.

'Taaaake him,' she wailed, turning her pinched eyes and pursed lips from the horror in her hands. She stretched a bundle of rocks towards the Inkling.

Spookasem had never seen Eulalie in such a state. Shocked, he took the lumps from her.

A distant buzzing that sounded like an angry wasp nest made him turn. A cloud of silver was making its way towards them, raining needles of light on the landscape,

'Eulalie, I'm not certain what those shiny things are, but I don't like them…hey… I thought you were carrying Rudolf?' he asked.

That set Eulalie off into a second storm of sobs, tempest of tears and gale of gasps.

'Imve klleddrol, Imme mrdr,' she spluttered.

'Shhhh, shhhhh, I have no idea what you said but I'm sure it's not that bad,' he tried to comfort her. Still holding the clump of rocks, he tapped her on her shoulder with an uncertain hand. 'Shhh…it…it's ok. It's not all that bad. Maybe…we should go…they're still after us,' he said. The buzzing of the cloud had now turned into a metallic whirring and was joined by shouts, curses and laughter. The Marauders were coming.

'Spookasem, it…it…it,' she hiccuped and choked on some after-tears. 'It doesn't matter if they catch me anymore. I'm a *murderer*, I've killed Rudolf.' She spoke those words with a terrifying finality – an honest, yet heart-wrenching admittance of guilt.

'You've killed Rudolf?' Spook repeated her shocked admission. He pulled his mouth in preparation for disgust and sneaked a peak at his hands. Curled up, head to the side and one little paw covering his nose, what *had* been Rudolf lay in his hands – not warm, soft and fluffy as he remembered – but cold, heavy and outlined with rough edges. His injured wing had completely broken off and it, too, lay between the Inkling's fingers.

Spook nearly screamed, but that would have made things even worse for poor Eulalie. So, he bit his scream back in a mere gasp for air. He did, however, nearly drop the gargoyle statue.

'Eulalie…no, you didn't…you're murderer…not. I mean you're not a murderer.' His mind knew what he wanted to say, but his initial shock had made him stumble over his words.

'I *am*. Look.' Her wet eyes stared unblinking at the wreck in his palms. She sniffed – but it didn't help the wet under her nose. He wished for a hanky, but instead, reluctantly offered her his flapping sleeve, which to his relief she denied with a mere shake of her head.

The Inkling's words had finally caught up with his thoughts. 'Eulalie, it's ok,' he said. 'Don't the stories say that it's normal? Gargoyles do…' Spookasem said, snatching at anything to make Eulalie stop sobbing.

Eulalie didn't hear a word he had said. She cried, 'I've killed something. I can't believe that I've actually killed something. I was just…' lines of spit pulled bars over her mouth, barring the rest of her words.

'Eulalie, listen,' Spook had to raise his voice. Stunned, she looked into his eyes and he imprisoned her stare. Droplets of lost tears clung to her eye-lashes. The buzzing of the Wind-ups now sounded angry. Every so often they would hear the creaking of cogs and springs as the Marauders wound up those that had run out of buzzing energy. 'Gargoyles *do* that. They turn to stone when they're injured or scared. This little one has lost a wing and was… is being hunted down. I'm surprised he hadn't turned to stone earlier.'

Eulalie searched his eyes for the lie, but there was none to be found. 'Are you sure?' She wiped under her nose. Something wet and green pulled across her cheek. 'Will he... how can I ...will he change back again?'

'Yes. I'm sure they do that. Goats fall over, octopuses squirt ink, lizards lose their tails, gargoyles turn into stone, lions...uhm...anyway, you get the point? We *really have* to go,' Spookasem said.

Eulalie's face changed instantly. The dark veil of horror dropped and was replaced by a shiny sprinkling of freckled strength, a sapling of hope and the beginnings of a plan.

In a swift movement, Eulalie had unslung the bag of gifts. She held the open flap towards the Inkling. 'Careful now,' she said.

The Inkling gently put the solid stone gargoyle – and the broken wing – into the bag.

'Ok. I have a plan,' Eulalie said. 'Let's go. We need to get to Knightsbridge as quickly as possible.

And just like that, all evidence of Eulalie's tears had disappeared – well, almost all. There was still a snail-trail glinting in a fine line from her nose to her cheek.

TWENTY-ONE

A GIANT WARRIOR'S SECRET

'If this works, then it will go down as the best idea we've ever come up with,' Spookasem said, tapping the giant statue's cheek as if it was a co-conspirator.

If Spookasem hadn't been so blinded by the excitement, he would have seen that Eulalie's ingenious ploy was actually just as full of holes as the net that was now flung over him. Having scored the main part, the Inkling had completely missed the fact that he was not only the star player, but also the main ingredient to a recipe for disaster. Eulalie had fought hard for the role, but the deciding factor had been the fact that the Marauders wouldn't be able to see Spookasem to shoot him, even if the Wind-ups could still detect him. Eulalie didn't possess such transparent luxuries and the hole in her boot was a stark reminder of that.

Now, Spookasem stood with one of the Marauder nets draped over his head and body and a length of fabric with drooping eye-holes strapped fast around his head. Sprinkled in Kahenna's shimmering red glare and splashed in ghastly shadows, Spookasem looked like *the* monster that lurked beneath beds.

'Lift your arms.' Eulalie held her hands in front of her mouth.

The Inkling stood right next to the large, gaping cave-of-a-mouth of Knightsbridge's yawning giant statue. He didn't respond to Eulalie's request. He just stood and stared at her, swaying slightly from side to side, like a sleeping ghost in the wind.

Maybe he hadn't heard her. 'Lift your ar…'

Spookasem hoisted his arms out to the side, lifting the draping net-sleeves like ghostly wings. He growled deeply and lunged at Eulalie. If her hand hadn't been pinching her lips tight in anticipation, she would have screamed – in fact, her cheeks bulged as the scream imploded. She stumbled back, tripping over her feet and landed on her bottom.

'Ha, ha, ha,' Spookasem laughed.

'You…you're terrifying,' she said and regaining her courage, she stood up.

'Thank you, thank you, ladies and gentlemen,' he teased and bowed to his invisible audience. 'Not even my best yet. I'm saving my greatest performance for the real thing.

'You know, Spook. I'm glad I'm on your side,' Eulalie said. 'Ok. Battle-stations. Let's give these Marauders a taste of their own medicine.'

Spookasem gave her a net-covered thumbs-up and disappeared behind the shrub that doubled up as the giant's side-burns. Eulalie double-checked his temporary camouflage and quickly sidled over the statue's lower incisors where the second part of their plan lay hidden. There, she inspected the twine that was hidden in the giant's cheeks and wound between his teeth like floss. All was in place. A hefty stick, about the length of her arm leaned against the tonsils. Now all they needed were some Marauders and a swarm of Wind-ups.

That, Eulalie knew, wouldn't take too long. Marauders were expert trackers – the stories said they could even track birds in flight, or see fish-prints in fading ripples. So, all they had to do was be patient and wait – and they didn't have to wait long either.

*

Click-clack-click-clack.

'Come on. Quick,' Eulalie said and bit her lip.

Click-clack-click-clack-click-clack.

'Come ooooon,' Eulalie said again.

She groaned, lifted her head and looked out of the giant's mouth. A handful of Wind-ups were hovering about fifteen paces away. Their humming was deafening. From the flashing silhouetted stems of the trees further on, it was clear that the bulk of their swarm was about to arrive – and with them the Marauders.

She ducked – and immediately a couple of thin lights probed the place her head had been moments earlier.

Click-clack.

'Finally,' she said. A brilliant spark spat into life and bounced from her flint and steel onto the fuel. That was all she needed. Moments later, she had woken up a lazy flame on the tip of a candle. She was huddled so close to it that it almost appeared as if she was whispering to the light – keeping it up to date with their plan.

Once the candle appeared satisfied with its role in this absurd mission, Eulalie stuck it to some wet wax on the tip of the giant's tongue. She then moved into the cheek. The whizzing and buzzing of all the Wind-ups sounded like a gale-force wind – she thought she heard voices too, but it was impossible to be certain. In any case, she was cornered now. It only occurred to her then that she had nowhere to run if anything went wrong.

Voices. Definitely, she thought. It was now or never. She adjusted the straps of the bag on her back, eyed the end of a knotted rope lying to her left and the club-like stick to her right.

Then she shuffled into the path of the candle's quivering light, allowing its brilliance to cast her very much enlarged shadow onto the back of the giant's mouth. Instantly, her shadow was drilled full of holes as dozens of little dots and lines of light followed that sudden movement. Eulalie screamed, ducked down and covered her head with her hands when arrows whistled into the mouth and shattered into splinters that rained down on her. Somehow, a little piece of wood even managed to end up in her mouth. She worked it with her tongue and spat it out in disgust.

'That was close, but I need you to come much closer. Spook, I hope you're ready. We'll only have one shot at this,' She whispered.

Eulalie waved her arms at the light, her movement magnified onto the wall as an enormous shadow. The noise of the Wind-ups echoed painfully in the confined space of the giant's mouth as they approached. More arrows whizzed past, bounced off stone teeth, tonsils and cheeks.

And then Eulalie ripped the end of the rope, releasing one of the Marauder's own nets that she and Spookasem had rigged on a rope between the gap in the giant's two large front teeth and his lower gums. The net stretched open, just as the bulk of the Wind-ups flew into the mouth. Strange whirring, snapping and almost comical *boings* of springs and coils replaced their loud buzzing and the whole mass collapsed in a knotted pile into the floor. Like fish in a net, some hopped about, still trying to lift off back into the air.

'Gotcha,' Eulalie said. She snatched up the stick, but she couldn't show herself yet. She was still a target. 'Come on Spookasem.' An arrow whizzed past her and pegged itself perfectly in a little gap in the mouth-cave right on her shadow's heart. Bits of stone crumbled in puffs of dust. A Wind-Up straggler limped into the cave and almost tentatively cast thin rays of light, before it ran out of energy and dropped straight onto Eulalie's head. A heartbeat later the screaming started.

It was quite the ensemble of different tones. The

performance started with Spookasem's high pitched wail, perfectly aimed at a ghostly tone that semi-quivered chain-like around the edges, while the drumming of his charging feet provided the epic rhythm.

Eulalie had to look – and she was glad she did, as it was a sight that would haunt her bedtimes with sudden fits of uncontrollable giggles for a long time afterwards.

Spookasem charged at the Marauders. He had his arms spread wide like wings and his legs were moving so fast that he appeared to be floating. The Marauders, of course, couldn't see the Inkling, just the mist-like form, draped in a ghostly veil chasing them down. Somehow, Spookasem managed to knit a vibrato into his voice that made it sound as if not one, but many banshees were bearing down on them from all sides. As Spookasem charged, the net snagged on brambles and shrubs which helped stretch out the fabric, making the Inkling look triple his true size.

One Marauder – Clarence, clearly identifiable by the brown stains on his tunic – screamed, but somehow no sound escaped his gut. At first Eulalie thought that it was the mask that was stopping the scream from coming out, but then in claustrophobic panic, he ripped it off his face. His whole body still appeared to be screaming; his eyes bulged, his mouth was gaping wide, far too wide to be humanly possible and his body was rigid and vibrating. It was only when Eulalie turned her head, that she realised that there was indeed sound, but it was so high that it was almost beyond her hearing.

When Clarence turned to flee, he was flattened by Adelaide, who managed to leave two perfect boot prints on his back.

Adelaide reached a handful of other Marauders at the edge of the line of trees as Clarence tore himself out of the mud and tumbled after her. By the time the group of newcomers had scrambled after them into the embrace of the trees, Eulalie had turned her attention to the Wind-Ups in the net.

Stick in hand, she hesitated. For a moment she felt sorry for them where they writhed and struggled, but then she reminded herself of Rudolf and how he, a living creature, had been chased by these machines and injured in the net. Pursing her lips, she lifted the make-shift weapon above her head. 'If I don't stop you now, you'll just be back another night when I'm not here to be the hero.' She swung it down with all her might.

TWENTY-TWO

THE BRUTISH SKISLES

'Maybe we should try a different tree. Remember that lone Bog Birch close to the mill? It drips sap all the time; it's very sticky too,' Spookasem said. He was still buzzing from the excitement of their successful ghostly plan. So excited, in fact, that he was still wearing his phantasmal outfit. He had at least pulled the net away from his face. Now it draped over him like a king's mantle.

Looking up from where he and Eulalie were kneeling, Spookasem scanned the swamp, calculating how long it would take him to get to the Birch and back again.

Stone Rudolf lay between Eulalie and Spookasem on a bed of leaves, his broken wing re-attached to his back. Painfully slowly, the wing tilted, re-opening the wound.

'You're right. It's not working. We need something else.' Eulalie sighed and bit her lip. 'I hope it doesn't hurt him.' The tree resin she had used to try and repair the little gargoyle shone like blood in the moonlight.

'By the moons,' she and Spookasem cursed together when

the wing slid from the wound and completely dropped off.

'Maybe if I push them together for longer.' Eulalie gently lifted the wing and Rudolf and pushed the two together again. She blew on it to try and hurry the drying of the sap.

'While you hold it, I'll run to the Birch and borrow some of his sap. It's the stickiest I know.' The Inkling didn't wait for Eulalie to respond but hopped up and darted off in the direction of the mill.

*

'That won't work,' a painfully familiar voice said.

Eulalie jumped up and took a few steps back. She felt Rudolf's wing separate from his body again when she pressed him protectively against her chest.

'You see. I told you it wouldn't work. Only glue would be able to sort that thing out,' Leroy said.

Eulalie couldn't see his eyes behind the mask, but she felt his stare burn into her. She had been so desperate to try and fix the wing before the little gargoyle pup woke that she had forgotten to open her senses to what was going on around her. She cursed under her breath. And who was this Glew he was talking about? Was he hidden in the trees with a crossbow pointing at her right now?

'I assume you *can* understand me, child. You did, after all, have quite a conversation with that useless Clarence, didn't you?' Leroy asked. 'We got off to a bad start, didn't we? Clarence really messed things up. Hello. I'm Leroy. What's your name?'

Eulalie didn't trust this sudden simpering friendliness. She searched his voice for anything that could give his intentions away.

Skilfully hidden behind an accent that she had never heard before, even in the tavern that was a magnet for travellers, she found an arrogant smugness and a very dangerous vein of a threat. With one hand she swung her sack onto one shoulder, her whole body wound up in flight mode.

'Don't run. Stay. Let's chat a while. This game is becoming a bit tedious. You *know* that I'd just hunt you down again. Let's make this easier for both of us,' Leroy said.

Eulalie's eyes darted to the crossbow that hung loosely in his hand and then at his boots. One can always tell by a person's boots and the way their feet and knees line up, whether the person would be a good runner or not. It was clear that he *was* indeed a very good runner.

They were halfway between Lancaster Gate and Marble Arch. In her mind she quickly found possible places to hide – there were many but she'd have to outrun Leroy first. But would that help? He would be able to track her down wherever she went.

'This scaring you?' Leroy turned his masked face to the crossbow – and threw the weapon to the side.

'I'm not scared of you. I'm not scared of anyone,' Eulalie said. She had loaded her voice thick with a red-hot courage that made it hiss like a hot poker stabbed into water.

'Finally,' Leroy said and lifted his hands to the side. 'You've not lost your voice somewhere in this god-forsaken place after all. Why…'

'Why are you hurting all the animals?' Eulalie interrupted him. 'They've done nothing to you.' Eulalie made her words bite.

'Oh my. Quite protective over these strange beasts, now aren't you? Are you a Crimson Shepherd perhaps?'

Eulalie didn't allow herself to be distracted by the fake compliment. She saw the shuffle he stole closer to her. She took it back and moved an extra one to make sure he could see that she had him sussed. She heard his snigger.

'Would you perhaps be so kind as to tell me why you are out here on such a dangerous night?' Leroy asked.

'I live here. This is my back yard. I can do what I want. At least I'm not hurting any anim...' Eulalie saw his weight shift back, like a cat ready to spring. She swirled around and scrambled away from him. He was much too fast for her though. When his hand grabbed the back of her neck, she whirled around and elbowed his arm so hard that his fingers tore free. She didn't get far.

Eulalie was brought to an abrupt halt. Her body was yanked backwards as her legs kept on running, until they, too, were lifted, one large boot managing to escape and land in a puddle of mud.

Still cradling the injured Rudolf stone, she slapped and kicked and tried to bite. Leroy avoided her blows quite effortlessly and transferred his hands from her bag to her collar.

'Only one's gonna get hurt and it ain't gonna be me,' he said through gritted teeth and shook her with such ferocity that the fight dropped out of her.

'That's better,' he said when she stopped aiming potential bruising his way. Pinning her down with her face to the ground, he pulled her bag free. Then he searched her pockets, removing anything he could find and finally ripped Rudolf and his severed wing out of her hands.

He left his foot on her back while inspecting her possessions.

'Give that back. It's mine,' she cried, but the embers of her fury had crumbled to ashes.

'Strange,' he said, ignoring her. He lifted Rudolf and inspected the broken wing. 'Like I said earlier. You'll need glue for this.' Stone Rudolf and his broken wing dropped inches from her face.

'Shell,' he scoffed. 'Useless.' It dropped by her nose.

Still pinned to the ground, Eulalie snatched up the shell and pocketed it.

'Where…where'd you get this?' Leroy asked, lifting up the tattered and torn remains of her *London Underground Mind the Gap Map*. 'Girl, the game's over. Tell me, *where* did you get this? And I can smell lies a mile away.' He lifted his foot and stepped back from her.

Eulalie recoiled. Lightning fast she snatched up Rudolf and his wing and stood up. Leroy's threatening aura faltered, his control diluted with sudden uncertainty. His masked face lifted from the map cradled in his hands to her face. 'Answer me, now,' he grunted.

'I…I found it. Here, in the swamp.' Eulalie tried to keep her voice steady and confident. 'It's a map of the swamp.'

'The swamp?' It sounded as if a bark and a laugh tried to squeeze out of Leroy's mouth at the same time. His large, mask-eyes looked at the map and then her again. Amusement was written in his every movement, the derogatory turn of his head and even the vapour-ghosts that clung to the vent-like openings of his mask.

'Any world through the eyes and imagination of a child is truly an entertaining place. Well and truly remarkable,' he said. It sounded as if he was talking to himself, though. 'This is not a map of the swamp. *This* is a map of the other side of what you people call the *Tempest-Barrier*.'

'You're lying to me,' Eulalie said. 'Nobody knows what Ketan looks like on the other side of the storms. No-one can get through.' Even though Eulalie hoped to prove the Marauder wrong, a very large part of her was hoping that he was actually correct. It would be a dream-come-true to know what lay beyond the storms.

'How ironic is this? Me, a stranger to your world; a mere red moon visitor and I'm educating *you* on what *your* world is all about,' Leroy said.

Leroy looked at his surroundings, as if gathering his thoughts. 'When that broken moon of yours – what is it that you call it? Kalani? - collided with your world, it *not* only created that impenetrable wall of storms that cut your world from north to south and south to north, but it *also* shattered the half of the world beyond the barrier into pieces. Those broken mountains, continents – are still there, but they aren't attached to this world anymore. Well, they're kind of attached… invisibly… by something called *gravitational force,* but that would be far too complicated for you to understand. The larger of these floating islands are called Skisles; as in Sky Isles.' He waited for Eulalie to respond. She didn't. She was already far away, drifting beyond storms with the islands and cliffs and boulders that hung in the sky like clouds.

'The Smaller ones that drift higher up are called Skighlands. And these … these drifting worlds…these ancient castles in the sky…' Leroy spread his arms in an effort to demonstrate their grandeur, '…together are called The Brutish Skisles. His voice was filled with such wonder that it almost sounded as if he had been there himself.

Eulalie wanted to believe him; she was desperate to believe him; she despised him, despised what he was doing to the animals in *her* swamp, but he had tapped into something huge, something fantastical – her imagination and *that* had her hooked instantly. His words dripped with the colours she so enjoyed and were filled with the sugary sweetness of certainty and conviction. She couldn't help *but* believe him. Her mind painted what he was describing on the canvas of her imagination and she was enthralled.

'Child, have you not heard that song *London Bridge is Falling Down?*' Leroy asked.

Eulalie nodded, her eyes wild; the pictures she was imagining shimmered and rumbled like a thunderstorm in their cinnamon depths. 'Uhm…London Bridge…falling down, yes,' she said. She knew the words. Everyone knew the words. But they were just gobble-di-gook, weren't they?

'What do they teach you at school? Do you even have schools around here? Appears *not*,' Leroy said, sounding as if he was truly enjoying himself. 'London Bridge was a miracle of design, an engineering feat that should not have been possible. It was a bridge built from this side of your world *over* the storms to the other side. It fell down millennia ago, but some remains still stand – and so does the song.'

Leroy was looking above Eulalie, his mind, too, soaring beyond the red-lined horizon. 'Don't you…haven't you ever wished you could know what is found beyond the storms?' he asked.

Eulalie nodded.

'Well, there are some people who believe that SoulGlass came from there. Magical SoulGlass that could be spun into thread to make flying carpets; ground into glass dust for hourglasses to wind back time and be blown into objects of immense power. I'm sure you would have heard of the stories of magic spinning wheels, all seeing mirrors, a sword that can slice into stone; and most powerful of them all, the SoulGlass Lanterns.' Leroy's eyes filled with greed and bulged with his every word. 'Yes, all those bed-time fairy-tales that are supposed to lull children to sleep are actually real. Every-single-one-of-them. And it all boils down to the magic of SoulGlass and...' his lobe-faced mask moved to his hands. 'And this map.'

Eulalie looked at stone Rudolf and his broken wing. 'How...how do I know you're not trying to trick me?' she asked.

'Why would I be here otherwise? Why would I spend a moment longer in a world where something is about to eat me around every corner? Do you know what riches await on the other side of the barrier? Don't you realise...'

'But why...' Eulalie looked at the broken wing.

'We are searching for a...' Leroy suddenly stopped as if he had almost said too much. He had been so drawn into his own story that he had got carried away. 'Look, child. Is this not proof enough?' He reached into his collar and slid out a gold chain that he wore around his neck. He held out a little stone about the size of a fingernail that was attached to the chain. Eulalie was about to say that it didn't prove anything, when he let go of it – and it floated. As if by magic, the stone lifted up and came to a rest right opposite his double snout. If it hadn't been for the chain, the stone would have floated away.

'Merciful moonbeams,' Eulalie whispered.

'Yes. You see. A piece of stone from the Brutish Skisles.' Catching it, he shoved it down the front of his collar. Unthinking, Eulalie clasped the glass playing cards that still hung around her neck. Somehow, Leroy had missed them when he had taken her belongings. He followed her fingers.

'What do you have there?' he asked.

Eulalie dropped her hand. 'Nothing.' *Nothing* – no matter how you say it, it almost always means the opposite. Now, it felt to her as if a bright pinpoint of light had illuminated her playing cards, highlighting to Leroy, and the rest of Ketan, that there was indeed *something* around her neck worth looking at.

'Let me see, child. Give those to me,' Leroy said. For a mere heartbeat, his confidence rocked into arrogance, which put him on the back foot. She snatched up her bag and swung it at Leroy. She missed him but hit his hand. Pieces of the map fluttered in all compass directions.

'The map, no,' Leroy shouted and dived for the first piece.

Without a moment's hesitation, Eulalie ran.

TWENTY-THREE
MOON PUDDLES

Eulalie's leg disappeared right up to her hip into a moon puddle. In full flight, her body came to a violent and wrenching halt. Rudolf, still just a clump of stone, was sent flying out of her hands as her body slammed forwards.

On any other night, she would have merely splashed across the puddle, disturbing only starry reflections. Kahenna's red stare, however, disturbed the unseen world, unsettling the natural order of things. It was as though her glow stretched, thinned, folded and frayed the fabric of space and time. Even shallow puddles could turn into enormous underwater worlds.

On all fours, Eulalie dragged her battered body a safe distance from the moon-puddle and then sat back to gather her senses.

Ruby puddles lay scattered around her like swamp freckles; a maze of reflections that resembled a large, broken mirror, with its pieces spread out like a jigsaw ready to be reassembled. *Bayswater*, she couldn't help but think of it that way, even though she now knew that the map had nothing to do with the swamp.

Eulalie's body was numb with shock and exhaustion and her bootless foot felt sore and swollen.

'Rudolf.' The stone gargoyle lay a few paces from her. His broken wing was lying neatly on the edge of a smaller puddle, balancing at an impossible angle between undergrowth and an unknown depth. Eulalie scrambled for it on her hands and knees, snatching it up, just before it slipped into the water.

In the moon's blushing light Eulalie caught sight of movement in the distance. 'Leroy,' she whispered. He wasn't running; it didn't even appear as if he was chasing her, merely taking a relaxing crimson moon stroll.

'My legs are so tired,' Eulalie whispered to herself. 'I can't run anymore.' She slapped her thighs to try and get life back into them again.

'Come on child,' Leroy called out. His voice hovered unwelcome in the wispy lines of mist that floated between them. 'I just want to look at that pretty necklace of yours.'

Keeping low, she crawled deeper among the scattered stepping stones of moon puddles, being careful to avoid tumbling into one again. When she and Spookasem had discovered that these puddles actually opened up during a crimson moon, they had spent hours lying on the edges, peering inside. They had both seen strange shadows that looked far too large *not* to be harmful. Even though a terrifying thought, Eulalie had vowed to explore them sometime. The Inkling promised never to talk to her again if she ever dared.

Eulalie eyed the puddle closest to her. Surely the monsters that lurked beneath couldn't be any more dangerous than the one stalking her now?

For a second time on the same night, she questioned the word *monster*. Maybe the answer lay there right in front of her. How many *real* monsters could the world contain? She already knew that Leroy was one.

Her fingers pulled Rudolf closer to her. He was solid and cold and yet she somehow felt that there was still life in there somewhere. She was going to have to trust the monsters to leave her alone for a moment, while she saved this little monster from the *real* monster.   Eulalie slipped her hat off her head and shoved it down her high collar; she yanked at the strap of her bag to make sure it snuggled into her. 'Spookasem is going to kill me if he knows what I'm going to do,' she smiled. Smiles had repelling properties; this one helped repel the fear that was drumming on her heart. 'Now, don't you struggle too much,' she whispered to Rudolf. Her lips gently touched his cold forehead. 'Don't be scared. Just stay close. You can close your eyes if you're too scared. Are you ready? Take a deep breath…'

Eulalie's breath whistled as she inhaled a bucket-full of mist and all the red air that her lungs could contain and snapped up a bit more, collecting it in her cheeks just for good measure. Without any second thoughts, she plunged head first into the mysterious and unexplored moon puddle. Kahenna squeezed her eyes shut in shock. She never expected that.

TWENTY-FOUR
A STRANGER TO A STRANGER WORLD

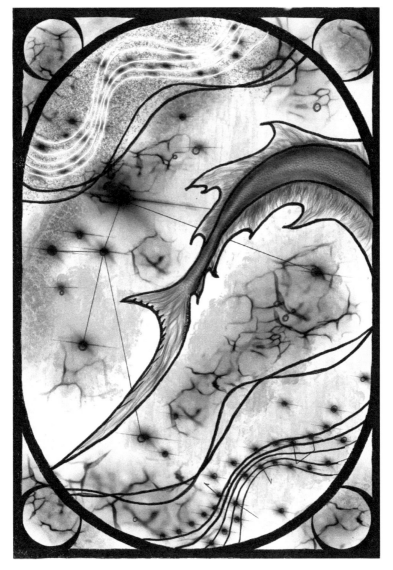

Eulalie cringed as the water bit at her with icicles for fangs. She forced her eyes open; the sudden cold and initial panic worked hard to try and steal all the air she had inhaled moments ago. Somehow, the cold had made the dark behind her eyes seem extra deep, so she needed to see around her.

A swarm of bubbles rushed past her, tickling her in their bouncy flight up to the surface. Her lungs complained about the lack of air – the groan sounded alien in her muffled surroundings.

Don't panic, don't panic, Eulalie thought.

She panicked.

Fear, dark and unknown cocooned her in a blanket of claustrophobia; her every instinct was screaming at her to breathe. Eulalie's legs battled the water, her boot and bag weighing her down. She pressed Rudolf painfully hard against her and stretched her free hand towards the surface as if reaching for something to pull her back up again. She didn't care about Leroy anymore; it didn't matter if he caught her; she just wanted to get out of the water.

Kahenna peeked through the lids of puffy clouds that had pulled past her.

The Marauder stood at the edge of the puddle, scratching his head. 'Surely, she couldn't just vanish into thin air?' Leroy asked himself.

Eulalie grabbed hold of a tuft of grass that dipped into the puddle. She was about to pull herself up through the thin, mirror-like door of the water, when she saw one of the most beautiful sights she had ever seen. Kahenna's red light burned a magnificent ray of crimson into the enchanted watery world. Eulalie's eyes followed the path of the ruby pillar as it illuminated the enchanted world beneath her. Peculiar eel-like fish twirled and twisted among a petrified forest of stalagmites; shadows with wings meandered past in a carefree watery flight; flashes of iridescent blue and brilliant white lit up the water-world in glittering constellations.

Eulalie let go of the grass and allowed the water to pull her away from the danger that stood a mere heartbeat from her.

'Child, you cannot hide forever.'

Leroy's muffled voice tore Eulalie's baffled gaze from her new world and she looked up. Inches from her she saw Leroy's outline quiver through her window of water. He appeared to be so close, and yet his distant voice made him appear small, insignificant and unimportant.

He doesn't know I'm beneath his feet; Eulalie's thought was followed by a cheeky smile that drifted up towards him in a bubble. She returned her attention to the world around her. As far as she could see, red beams of light shone through puddle-windows piercing this cavernous underwater world. It reminded her of the sun rays that cut through the holes in the roof of her mill.

Without the urgent pressing of panic on her chest, Eulalie felt more at home in the water. Using her free hand and feet, she turned and kicked, then allowed the smooth hands of the water to guide her to one of the other moon-puddle windows. There, she drifted to the surface.

Steam billowed from her wet hair when her head broke through the watery curtain into the night air. It was only when she took her first breath, that she realised that she had felt almost as comfortable in the water as her own world. Aside from the urge to gasp in a breath, there had been something else; the bubbles in the water had prickled her skin. She had almost imagined that she could have drawn them in through her pores for breath. Did everyone feel like that in water?

Eulalie blinked the waviness out of her eyes. And what she saw, wasn't a pretty sight. Leroy's legs bridged the puddle she had floated up through. He must have moved while she was aiming for this moon window.

'Madigan, Madigan,' he shouted. The thin veil of jest and friendliness that had clothed his voice earlier had been lifted and he now sounded as harsh and awful as his intentions. 'I will find you. This game you're playing has just taken a dangerous turn. You can't hide from me forever.' His boot clipped the edge of her moon puddle. 'There's nowhere in this world that is safe for you anymore. My patience has run out,' he shouted.

I'm not playing, Eulalie thought. She stole a quiet breath and allowed her wet burdens to pull her back into the water.

Unseen to her, a shoal of large shadows darted between the beams of light far beneath her, avoiding being touched by the invading light-columns. The creature swimming in front suddenly stopped. With arms stretched wide and a long, muscular tail swaying beneath him, he hung suspended in the water. His senses had picked up a strange vibration. Far above him, close to one of those holes that unlocked when the red moon was out, he saw a child from the world above floating in the water. The vibrations were coming from her; not wild, frantic vibrations fuelled by panic or drowning, but fish-like; in the way the impulses of water-life connected to the surroundings.

'Go. I'll follow soon,' he sang to the others in their language of hums and clicks. Then he glided into an especially dark shadow directly opposite where the girl hung suspended.

'What are you?' he crooned, when he realised that he wasn't the only one curious about this strange child. She had drawn quite the crowd. The shadows around her were bursting with a very peculiar audience. A pre-school outing of selkie pups were doing a May-pole dance around her shadow; three sea-horse-unicorns were pecking the dirt off the child's bare foot and two frog-princes and a princess were making crowns of anemone-chains using the bubbles that had stuck to her clothing.

'I need to see your face,' he whisper-sang. He pulled down his hood of kelp and shadow and swam around her. His eyes followed the constellation of stars on her skin, the perfect outlines of snowy lakes, stepping-stone dots that led his gaze to her eyes... he recoiled and nearly cried out when he saw the secrets that swam in the otherworldly depth of those eyes.

*

The mermenin stayed until the child finally exited his world; he had even held out his hand when she kicked to try and pull herself out of the water. Gently he had allowed her to step on his open palm and had even given her a little push, quickly hiding again when she had looked down to see what she had kicked against. For a long time afterwards he had stayed, just to make sure that she didn't come back again. When he had finally left and swam after his friends, he hadn't realised, but he had been holding his hand to his chest, searching for comfort from his wildly beating heart.

TWENTY-FIVE
NO MORE HIDING PLACES

'Are you sure that's what he said?' Spookasem could hardly believe what Eulalie had just told him. 'Floating worlds? Castles in the sky?'

The walls of the old mill stopped creaking for the moment, as if it, too, held its breath while drifting away on the wings of such wondrous thoughts.

'Yes. Definitely. He even laughed that I thought that it was a map of the swamp,' Eulalie said. Her eyes gleamed at the impossibility of it all. She gently dropped Rudolf into her bag and swung it around her shoulders. 'He said it happened when Kalani crashed into our planet.' She then untied *Hocus Pocus*, who had been waiting patiently in the water tunnel under the mill where she had left her earlier in the evening. Eulalie turned her eyes to the dark ceiling, searching the moss and algae stalactites for any intrusion of light from the room above. There was none. *Beware the wind that blows* … her eyes glanced over those strange words as she turned back to her boat.

'Here, help me with this,' Eulalie said. She groaned and leaned back against the boat's weight. With the Inkling's help, she managed to pull the skiff to the opposite wall where the scoop wheel rocked gently in the water.

'It's darker on this side. Even if Leroy searches the mill and peers down one of the spaces between the floor boards, he still won't be able to see us,' Eulalie said.

'Wow. Just imagine,' Spookasem whispered. 'Floating worlds. What I wouldn't give to be able to see them. What were they called again?'

'Sky Isles. Skisles. And yes, me too,' she answered.

'And the little stone around his neck was *actually*

floating…?' Spookasem asked just as footsteps thundered above them.

'Shhh. Shhh.' Eulalie pushed her finger to her lips and pulled Spookasem down. 'Quick. Let's tilt her.' With a silent struggle, they angled *Hocus Pocus* until it nearly tipped, but came to a rest against the scoop wheel, making a perfect cave for them to hide in.

'There, look,' Eulalie said and pointed.

Lines of amber cut through the gaps in the floor boards above them, so bright that it almost seemed as if the room above them was on fire.

The light bullied the shadows into hiding as a mere few feet above them, the intruder carrying the lantern walked. Booming drumbeats invaded their wet chamber.

Eulalie and Spookasem huddled together in *Hocus Pocus'* shadow-cave.

Another light appeared. This one shone with a white brilliance.

'SoulGlass? How can you be sure?' a man asked.

Eulalie didn't recognise that voice. Tapping footsteps drowned out the first part of the reply.

'… I know *M*. I just have this gut feeling. I know it's just a hunch, but I'm certain it was SoulGlass.' That was Leroy's voice and he was speaking to someone he called *M*. This must be that mysterious *M* the Marauders mentioned; the one they all seemed to be so afraid of.

A rough square shadow settled in the boards above Eulalie and Spookasem. The Marauders above them must be standing directly on the mat that hid the trapdoor. The dirty old rag was tracing a shadow imprint on the wood.

'Wars were fought over SoulGlass,' *M* said. It's far more precious than diamonds. It's so rare that most now believe it a myth and you're telling me that we've got to follow your *gut?* Follow a *hunch?' M* didn't sound convinced.

Leroy mumbled something that Eulalie couldn't make out.

M continued. 'Hundreds of years ago, people in this world were hunted down and murdered when someone had a *hunch* their souls were made of this magical glass. They were almost always wrong. If we were to pursue this and you were wrong, Leroy, it would not end well for you.'

'But *M*. I know it's almost impossibly unlikely, but can we afford *not* to find out?' Leroy asked. 'Think of what the great glassblowers of old created after they melted those rare few glass souls they *did* find. Items that could topple kingdoms, rule worlds. Every single fairy-tale in existence grew from the history of those SoulGlass artefacts.'

Eulalie listened in awe. Leroy's story was nothing new to her. Most of her fairy-tale books *were* about those stories. Very often, however, the barrier between those fables and her mundane reality became wider with the closing of a book. The way these Marauders were speaking about SoulGlass just made it all seem so real.

'Show me that map you mentioned,' *M* said.

Whoever this *M* was, he most certainly had a dangerous authority – a presence that made even Leroy cower. They heard him fumble with the map.

'Mmmm, yes,' *M* said. 'Definitely a map of the Brutish Skisles. And this faerie-child you've mentioned found it here in the swamp?'

Eulalie frowned and turned her head to Spookasem. *Faerie child?* They thought that she was a faerie. Still frightened, Eulalie couldn't help feel a flame of pride. She didn't mind being confused with the Fey.

That means someone got through the Tempest Barrier, *M* said. You see, my friend. It *is* possible. That puts an urgency in our search. Maybe someone at that tavern knows something about this. What's that stench pit called again?' he asked.

'Uhm. Madigan. She said her name was…' Leroy answered.

'Not the child, stupid. The tavern.' *M* laughed.

'Oh…sorry…the tavern's called *The Cross in the Roads,*' Leroy muttered. Someone shuffled about. Shadows shifted.

'Apparently, it's quite the enchanted place,' Leroy said. He sounded very pleased to be the wielder of so much knowledge about the tavern. 'Remember that Crimson Shepherd we captured last time we were out here?' he asked.

'Hmm.'

Eulalie didn't know whether *M* answered or if he just blew his nose.

'Well,' Leroy said. 'After a bit of… what can I call it…prodding, he mentioned a few interesting things. Apparently, hundreds of years ago; long before the first brick of the tavern had even been placed, four SoulGlass lanterns hung on four pillars in exactly the same place where the tavern now stands. Travellers who didn't manage to find a place to hide before the red moon showed her ugly face on a red night, like this one, would find shelter in the halo of light cast by those lanterns. They even had this silly rule that everyone became equal in the light of those lanterns. Slave traders had to unshackle their slaves; criminals shared the light with their captors as free men and the rich shared their wealth with the poor while blanketed by the lantern's light. Those lanterns are gone now and only two of the original pillars still stand. Apparently, a washing line now. That's where the tavern was built and gets its name from: *The Cross in the Roads.*' Leroy's voice wove the name of the tavern in a tapestry of wonder.

A long, terrifying silence followed.

'*The Cross in the Roads,* you say? Four SoulGlass lanterns that cast protective light?' It sounded as if *M* was thinking out loud. 'The power of even one of those lanterns is unimaginable...but *four*? Find this child.' *M* suddenly barked. 'If she lives under this cursed moon, she'll almost certainly know how to get past the enchantments that prevent us from getting to the tavern. Our plans have now changed. I have some important matters to attend. You are to stay here until you find this child or the lanterns or a way to get to this *Curse in the Roads*; preferably all three. Don't even dare returning empty handed. I shall not be disappointed, now, shall I?'

'Yes, *M*,' Leroy answered. 'I mean no. I won't disappoint.' He didn't sound very pleased at the idea of staying under Kahenna's brutal stare much longer.

'You might need this,' *M* said. 'Now just be careful with it. Only use it if absolutely necessary. If you shoot someone... anything with this, there won't be much left to pick up afterwards. You put the gunpowder and ammunition in there; point it in the general direction of whatever you want to blast, then pull that trigger.' Whatever it was sounded terrifying, but there was a fine sprinkling of humour in *M's* voice – pride almost.

'Th… thanks,' Leroy replied.

'Ok, I'm off,' M said. Sudden loud footsteps made Eulalie shove her hands to her ears and she made herself small against the scoop wheel. A door slammed.

In the absence of the white light, the lines of amber above Eulalie and Spookasem now appeared feint. The light lifted and once again it moved, making the shadows shuffle away. Rude and uninvited, thin strings of Leroy's lantern momentarily found Eulalie and Spookasem's hideout, highlighting the sharp angles of fear on their faces.

The light dimmed and shadows rushed back to their rightful places. Eulalie slumped and almost slid into the water as relief replaced the oppressing weight of terror.

All of a sudden, the footsteps rushed back to the middle of the floor. Eulalie was too late to stop her whole scream from escaping; part of it made it through her fingers when the square of shadow above them was flung aside.

*

Far above the mill, the stars between the smoky duet of the colliding galaxies and Kahenna, covered their eyes in horror. They had been watching, holding their breaths. One of those stars, a very feint, insignificant little pin-prick of a speck in the night sky blinked. It not only terrified for the girl with the beautiful map on her face and her strange friend, but also for another child who was much closer to it – a child who, too, was hiding – and just like the child hidden in the mill, this other child's hiding place had also been discovered.

TWENTY-SIX
FATHER CHRISTMAS IS NOT REAL

'For the life of me. The holiday's only just started and I'm already wishing for the new term to begin. She's nearly ten. It's about time she grows up. Just tell your sister to get out of the cupboard,' the man said and leaned closer to the computer screen.

'Dad, I *have*. Sireneya just refuses. She says there's a monster under her bed,' the boy said. He shifted his weight from foot to foot and kept glancing back up the stairs. For just a moment he wanted to remind his dad that she was nearly *nine*, and *not* ten and that it was still a perfectly good age to be a child. He didn't want his little sister to get into trouble, but he couldn't leave her in the cupboard. What if she suffocated?

'Then tell her monsters aren't real.' The boy's dad sighed and leaned back into the groaning chair. The blue light of the screen highlighted the tired lines under his glazed eyes. Shaking his head, he removed his glasses and rubbed the bridge of his nose. 'I really have to finish this email,' he said.

That's what his dad had said about two hours earlier. A strange feeling of déjà vu reminded the boy that his dad had also said it the day before. Today was Christmas Eve; who would be doing work the day before Christmas?

'I'm sorry, Reyn. I'm just so busy. Didn't mean to sound upset. I'll come.' Without straightening up, Reyn's dad stood, unable to shift the weight of whatever he had been busy with from his shoulders. He paused for just a moment next to Reyn, put his hand on his son's shoulder and then shuffled up the stairs.

*

'Siren?' the man asked and knocked on the cupboard door. 'Sirene? There's no monster under your bed. I've checked.'

Reyn shared the doorway to his sister's room with the

shadows cast by her nightlight. The flickering lights of the Christmas tree also managed to sneak in from downstairs – there was quite the crowd gathering in Sireneya's cluttered room. A red light flashed as it spotlighted a row of books stacked under a mounted wand; blue and yellow lights raced to claim the series of books on the windowsill while purple and green lights flickered as they bickered to make it to the ship that popped out of the pages of the book lying open on a desk.

'You didn't check.' Sireneya's distraught voice barely made it through the cupboard door.

'I did…' their dad turned around and sidled to her bed. He didn't have to sigh – his whole body did that for him.

Reyn couldn't help but smile. He could just imagine his sister sitting there in the dark cupboard, arms folded and lower lip rolled down in defiance.

His dad leaned onto the bed and helped himself onto his knees. Giving his son a *what-are-you-smiling-at* look, he flung aside Sireneya's Gryffindor duvet and ducked under the bed. Moments later, his head popped back. 'Ok. I've checked. There's no monster under your bed,' he called, feeling quite stupid to be talking to a cupboard.

'It might be invisible,' Sireneya answered in her cupboard-muffled voice.

Once again Reyn's dad disappeared. The boy shook his head when he heard his dad tap the floor.

'There. I've searched. The monster is *not* invisible,' his dad said, stood up and walked back to the cupboard. He pulled at the handle. Sireneya must have been holding the door from the other side. He rattled the door. 'Sireneya.'

Oh dear. His dad never called his sister by her full name unless it was serious.

'Did you hear me? I felt under the bed. There is *no* monster and it's *not* invisible. Come out now,' his dad said.

'What if...what if...what if it's not there yet, but waiting for midnight? What if there's a door? Under the carpet. And it only opens at midnight and then the monster climbs out to eat me from my toes to my head?' Sireneya asked.

Reyn stifled a laugh.

'Sireneya...'

'Monsters love midnight,' she interrupted her dad. 'That's when they're strongest. Long fingernails and green slime dripping out of their noses...like a goblin. Or a boggart. Boggarts are terr...'

'Sireneya. That's enough. I don't know who or what has been filling your head with such nonsense...' Their dad's eyes circled her room while his voice trailed away. The answer to his question peered back at him from every bookshelf, wall and even the ceiling.

'Monsters aren't real,' their dad said, more as an afterthought. His conviction had been drained by the sudden uselessness he felt. Then he kindled some anger. This was wasting time. He had emails to send. 'Sireneya.' *That* sounded better. 'Monsters. Aren't. Real.' He slammed his flat hand against the door.

'They are,' Sireneya shouted back.

This time Reyn covered his eyes. His sister was pushing her luck.

She continued her reasoning. 'If the Easter Bunny is

real…if Father Christmas is real, then monsters are also r…'

'They're not. They're *not* real. They're *all* just silly stories to help entertain children like you. I've had enough of this time-wasting game. You come out of the cupboard this very minute. I am in two minds to cancel Christmas. I shall not ask again,' their dad said. His tone left no room for any arguments.

Reyn heard his sister gasp. From his dad's body language, he could see that he knew he shouldn't have said that. It was too late though. The door swung open and shadows scurried for cover. What was said couldn't be taken back. His dad was going to have to see this one through.

Sireneya burst through the waterfall of clothes. Sidestepping her dad, she dived onto her bed and with a hop, she had flicked the duvet from under her and cocooned herself in it.

His dad stormed out of the room.

The day before Christmas. Why did things always crumble the day before Christmas?

When he could hear his dad's anger tapping out on the computer keyboard, he went and sat down on the side of his sister's bed. Could he pick up the pieces? Where to begin?

'Sirene…'

'Go away.'

He put his hand on her covered shoulder. Before she shrugged his touch away, he could feel that she was crying.

He stood up and looked at the poster of Sireneya's idol. The girl wizard stood poised, pointing her wand towards an unseen enemy. Not for the first time, Reyn wished that he could just swing a wand and make things all better.

He walked out of his sister's room. He could go and put

away the Father Christmas suit now. There would be no need for it in the morning. Father Christmas had just been revoked. At least it was supposed to snow soon. His sister loved snow. Hopefully that would lighten up an already miserable Christmas.

TWENTY-SEVEN
BEWARE THE WIND

'Spookasem, he's found us.' Eulalie grabbed for the Inkling; her fingernails cut into his shoulders. She couldn't tear her eyes from the brightening light above them. They could see Leroy's shadow pushing the light aside as he searched for the latch. Eulalie heard his voice, but his words were just another drumming in her ears.

'We've got nowhere to go. We're trapped and there's …' Something in the thick walls creaked, frightening the rest of her words away. It felt as if the mill itself was taking a deep breath, waking like a hibernating beast of the blood moon. Eulalie's eyes glanced over the wall to see whether she could see where this new, terrifying noise was coming from, but saw only *Beware*…tattooed into the stone.

'Eulalie, stay calm. We could…' the Inkling tried. He was normally quite good at coming up with spur-of-the-moment plans. Urgency had always been a wonderful catalyst for sudden get-us-out-of-here-ideas. This time, though, nothing came to him.

The trapdoor above them lifted, but before it yawned too wide, Spookasem leaped for the latch rope and snatched it in mid-air. Like a monkey swinging on a vine, the Inkling's legs swung forwards, his bodyweight snapping the door out of Leroy's hands.

'I've got it…' Spookasem shouted, but mid yodel, he slipped, tumbled and half disappeared under the water.

Eulalie pulled him up by the collar and out of the way.

A heart-beat later, the door flung open and slammed mercilessly into the wall. Eulalie screamed, let go of Spookasem and covered her head with her arms as a thick, heavy beam of light stormed into their hideout.

'The boat,' Eulalie shouted. 'Get behind it.' *M*'s words

about the terrifying weapon he had handed to Leroy still echoed uninvited in her mind.

Both she and Spookasem dived to find cover behind *Hocus Pocus*, but Eulalie fell against it and the boat toppled back into the water, rocking and swaying.

'Eulalie, get in. Get into the boat and duck down. Leroy might shoot,' Spookasem shouted. Eulalie rolled over the gunwale just as Spookasem pushed.

'By the moons.' Spookasem cursed. 'I forgot she's full of holes. Get out. She's gonna sink…'

A deep *creek*, followed by two, three, four hollow *clunks* vibrated through the thick walls, even shaking the floor beneath their feet.

'I told you that you can't hide from me,' Leroy shouted. He leaned through the trapdoor, lantern dangling in his hand. 'You wanted to make things diff…' The whole building shook, making him drop his words – and nearly his lantern too. Something enormous groaned deep, like a monster stretching stiff bones. More *clacks* and *clunks* played percussion on the mill's walls while unseen chains shook like an angry ghost.

Eulalie swung around to the trapdoor, but instead of seeing Leroy, her eyes found those strange words. A flood of light had spilled into the scraped font. *Beware the wind that blows from where the red moon rises.*

Outside, the wind changed and the sails of her mill swayed and moved. Breaking the confines of splintered wood, old rust and exhaustion from days of old, the sails circled into a tentative cartwheel. Testing its strength and reminding itself of how wonderful it felt to move, the mill sent out an almighty groan, rumbling into the night.

The mill shook and plaster cracked and tumbled down onto Eulalie and into *Hocus Pocus*. 'Spook,' Eulalie shouted and covered her head. 'Where are y…?'

'I'm holding up the boat,' she heard his voice from somewhere beneath her. 'Too many holes. I don't have enough fingers to plug them all up,' he shouted. 'I'm gonna try my toes.'

Moss and algae lifted like hag heads out of the water when the scoop wheel turned. Eulalie gripped the splintered gunwale as her boat rocked and swayed at the mercy of the waves' impatient hands. Spookasem's efforts were lost amid the powerful forces at work. Leroy shouted something, but creaks, groans and the clacks of the wooden cups drowned out his words.

A sudden surge thrust *Hocus Pocus* deeper into the water tunnel, where it turned in a slow circle and sank even deeper into the dark. Spookasem lost his grip and disappeared face first under the inky water.

'Madigan,' Leroy shouted.

Eulalie looked back at the sound of Leroy's voice, but she couldn't find him. Her eyes involuntarily searched for something familiar – anything that could help her get out of this nightmare. *… the wind blows … the … moon rises,* was the last thing she saw as her boat swung in a circle and disappeared into the water, pulling her down with it.

'Eulalie. Eulalie!' Spookasem splashed and pulled at the water to get to the place where *Hocus Pocus* had gone down. Waves spluttered into his eyes and mouth and the current created by the scoop wheel forced him deeper into the tunnel towards the sluice gate. 'Where are you? Where are you?' he shouted as his legs searched for the boat that had not only sunk but appeared to have been swallowed up by the ground beneath.

'What witchcraft is this?' the Inkling shouted at Leroy who had now also stepped into the water and was wading to the same spot. 'What have you done with Freckles?'

Leroy, of course, couldn't see or hear the Inkling. Holding his lantern aloft, the Marauder approached the place where Eulalie had vanished. Tens of dozens of bubbles clutched each other amid the dark ripples. These were the only flotsam that indicated there had even been a boat; he felt around with his feet, just in case there was perhaps a deep depression that could hide a boat and a person.

The scoop wheel was now turning with renewed joy and Leroy was battling the current. Finding nothing under the water, he leaned into the current and waded backwards towards the ramp. 'I knew it,' he said to himself. 'SoulGlass magic, definitely.'

Spookasem gulped a lungful of air into his lungs and dived into the pitch-black dark. Where was Eulalie? What would happen if the ink on her hand washed off? What if she died? He would never know what had happened to her. He patted around in the slimy carpet of muck on the canal bed, but found nothing, except algae that slipped under his fingernails.

Two, three times, he went up to borrow more air. Finally, bumped and bruised and shivering with the cold, he used the last of his strength to battle the flow of the water and crawl up the ramp. 'Eulalie,' he said. His breath came in cloudy gasps and barely made it through the cold wisps that clung to his lips. Still up to his waist in the water, he turned back to where Eulalie had disappeared. 'Freckles. Where are you? Where are you?' he called.

Movement on the wall right next to him caught his eye. 'Beware the wind that blows from where the Red Moon rises,' he read the words, while his water-wrinkled, shivering fingers traced the scraped font. *Beware the wind,* he whispered; or rather thought he whispered. He wasn't focusing on the words anymore, but the tiny dust-specks of ruby light that vibrated up and down the mysterious warning. A deep, almost inaudible *whoosh, whoosh, whoosh,* accompanied the glittering moon-glow as if the mill was breathing and its heart was beating in time to the turning of the wheel.

TWENTY-EIGHT
DOWN THE CHIMNEY

Hocus Pocus burst through an explosion of shattering glass as if there had been a hidden window at the bottom of the canal. Eulalie's beloved skiff swung sideways as she dived for cover and pinched her eyes shut to avoid the razor pieces of glass she expected to cut her to pieces. None came. Her skiff just turned in dizzying circles through a strange, thick liquid that flowed like honey but tasted like burnt wood and pressed in on her from all sides. Having somehow avoided the broken glass, she stretched her arms out to grasp on to both sides of the gunwale. She couldn't move or do anything but wait for the nightmare to be over. She didn't know how long she would be able to hold her breath for.

All of a sudden, *Hocus Pocus* bumped against something with a hollow clunk that nearly jolted Eulalie out of the boat. Wincing, she shook her head from side to side, but she couldn't resist the urge to breathe any longer. Her back arched and she breathed in violently. Bubbles of air broke free from the heavy liquid inside her nose and mouth and flowed into her lungs. Unable to get the air into her lungs quick enough, she gasped and chewed at her surroundings. Relief washed over her in wave after wave of goosepimples. She could breathe.

Moments later, frozen gusts of wind replaced the liquid and the icy fingers of the air clawed at her wet skin. Snowflakes were playing hide-find-seek with the wind; they dashed about in upward spirals, horizontal bursts and explosions of white. *Hocus Pocus* creaked and a plank of wood cracked. She wasn't sinking any longer but was being juggled between a merciless circus of clouds and the drunken hands of the wind.

The hull scraped on something. It sounded as if she had

just sailed over rocks. Her poor skiff teetered for a moment and then plunged down a slope. Eulalie screamed. Just as she thought she was plummeting to her death, two dark towers pillared out of the swirling clouds of snow ahead of her, one screaming dark smoke into the storm-clouds. *Hocus Pocus* crashed to a halt against the other pillar.

Cowering in the bottom of her boat, Eulalie protected her head with her arms. 'By the moons,' she breathed. For a few moments she lay like that, waiting for the agony.

'F… fingers…' she balled her hands. 'Nothing broken,' she whispered.

'Spookasem? Are you still here?' she whisper-called, but only the wind answered.

'Owww, my ribs.' She pressed onto the ache and took an expanding breath. 'Ok. It's ok. Just tender.' Some naughty flakes of snow tickled their way into her nose and mouth. 'Spookasem,' she called louder, trying her best to compete with the wind.

Gripping the side, Eulalie peered over her little wall of wood. *Hocus Pocus* groaned. 'By the blessings of the four moons,' she whispered – or she thought she whispered. Her lips made the movements, her mind formed the words, but the wind stole every sound.

Eulalie couldn't believe what she was seeing. 'I'm. On. A. Roof,' she said to the snow, who was obviously totally aware of that. Eulalie looked about. She was stuck between a chimney and the steep angle of the roof tiles. Behind her was another chimney. In fact, whatever she had landed on had two more. All of them were sending out waves of smoke, except the one she was wedged against.

'Now, don't buck,' she said and patted *Hocus Pocus*' side. Satisfied, Eulalie sidled out of the boat. 'My foot. It's so cold,' she said. An icy gust sliced a chill through her wet clothes and her hair seemed to pull at her scalp. An army of ant-like goosepimples attacked her skin. She needed shelter or she'd freeze.

'H…how c…c…c…can I g…g…get off the roof?' she asked. Through the blizzard she could just make out the tops of more roofs and a forest of chimneys, but they were all too far away from her to be useful.

Eulalie's shivering shifted from shuddering waves to a continual, relentless storm-surge of shakes. She hugged her arms around her chest, shoving her hands into her armpits. But numb and cold, she couldn't feel any heat in them anymore. *What in the name of Ketan is going on? How have I ended up on a roof?* She knew all about getting lost in the red moonlight, but she had never imagined anything like this. And the cold came much too fast. Only a few heartbeats earlier, she had been under the red glow of an Autumn Kahenna.

'S… sss…S…ppp…p…p…Poop …asem.' Eulalie's lips were moving of their own accord. Cold had stolen even her words. Had Kalani, the shattered moon, perhaps managed to bully her way past Kahenna, spraying the world with her frozen tears? Squinting, she looked up, but the sky was hidden by a thick blanket of clouds. Her eyes ventured back to the chimney. She had no other choice.

TWENTY-NINE
SANTA IS A GIRL

Sireneya lifted her head very carefully from behind the sofa and searched the living room. The fading and brightening of the Christmas lights played havoc with the shadows and everything appeared to have sprouted reaching arms and legs.

The lampshade stood at attention in the corner; its head bowed low, gnarled arms hanging by its side. It seemed to stand vigil at the lament of Father Christmas' demise. Next to it stood *flat screen,* the TV. Hardly ever used, a layer of dust powdered its grey face; someone had given the dust a token wipe, leaving imprints of lopsided eyes and a gaping, screaming mouth staring at her. Even the vase of stale water and wilting flowers on the side cabinet had come to life. Bent over and hunch-backed, the zombie flowers peered at her under spiny brows and a failing flower hairline.

The Christmas tree, at least, stood tall and proud next to the inglenook fireplace – empty of fire, but shimmering in the yellows and oranges of the fairy lights.

The monsters had been making so much noise, that Sireneya had thought they must be eating roof-tile sandwiches. How was it possible that her dad had not heard that? There was no point waking him to tell him that the monsters were in fact, not under her bed, but clambering over the house. If he didn't believe her about the creatures under the bed, he wouldn't believe her about the ones outside either.

If it hadn't been for the thought of being buttered onto a monster sandwich, she would have dared searching out the help of her brother. The only problem was, that his room was the converted attic – and would be the first place the monsters would arrive once the roof tiles were eaten through.

Reyn wasn't bad at all. He would believe her. He was in danger now. She'd have to go and warn him. Sireneya grabbed for the courage that lay draped at her feet and lifted it up like heavy shield. She was about to dart for the stairs when an almighty crash in the unused hearth made her scream and she ducked back down behind the sofa.

Biting her hand to force a second, louder scream back to where it was trying to escape, she glared at the lump lying in the old soot. A body. Someone – or rather the remains of someone - had just dropped down the chimney. Little specks of dust still hovered around it like flies around a carcass. Tentative snowflakes followed it down and settled like a veil over the disgusting remains.

'What do I do, what do I do, what do...?' Sireneya inhaled a little squeak when sinister scraping, hollow mumbling and eerie cursing escaped the mouth of the chimney. Something was coming down the chimney. It was the monster. It was searching out the warmth of her house to finish off its feast of blood and bones; and then maybe have her for dessert.

Sireneya's imagination was totally out of control and was rushing through amber lights and jumping the red ones in its race to reach panic.

If only they had made a fire in that hearth. Her dad had said that it was too close to the Christmas tree and the stockings. She was up for moving them, but he didn't want to. He had an email to finish. *Why does he never listen to me?* she thought, her quivering lips shaking and tears collecting in her lashes.

The snow that drizzled down into the fireplace turned black with soot and was joined by bits of brick and a foot.

A foot. A bare foot not much larger than Sireneya's swayed

once, twice, three times like the pendulum of a wall clock. Moments later, the whole body crashed down and landed with a painful hiccup in an explosion of dust, more soot, a tumble of clothing – and red curly hair.

Sireneya ducked for cover. Clutching one hand to her mouth, the other to her chest, she begged her heart to slow down. And then the monster sneezed and sniffed. Sireneya held her breath. Another sniff; no munching of flesh or crunching of bones as she had expected.

Sireneya crawled to the edge of the sofa and peered around it, expecting the last thing she would ever see to be a gaping mouth, riddled with fangs as it dislocated its jaw to swallow her whole. Instead, the world she knew shook, turned a wild circle and nearly crumbled around her. It wasn't a creature from her worst nightmares making its way out of the fireplace, but Santa Claus – and Santa wasn't a man, but a girl.

*

With one bare foot and one large booted one spread-eagled in front of her, Eulalie waited for the stars of confusion and cramping muscle shivers to disappear. She must have bumped her head harder than she thought when she tumbled those last few feet. Her hand searched her forehead, then the back of her head, but found no bumps, just soot, dust and a bird's nest of hair. She shoved her hand down her high collar, pulled out her flat cap and flopped it onto her hair in an effort to tame the tangle.

Still the lights flickered and the shadows danced in a dizzying waltz. Eulalie closed her eyes, rubbed them with her knuckles and then pinched the bridge of her nose.

A beautiful warmth washed over her in waves; she breathed deeply, savouring the air perfumed with open fires and a feint hint of spiced apple.

A sneeze shook her back to her senses. 'By the moons. My bag. Something crunched when I fell on it,' she said and rolled off her bag, pulling it out from under her. To her relief, she had missed Rudolf and his broken wing – they were still intact; well sort of – separated, but intact. She pinched her presents and found the broken one. 'Oops. Sorry,' she whispered into the bag.

Even though solid rock, she carefully laid the gargoyle and the broken wing on the floor next to the hearth and straightened up. For a moment she savoured the relaxing warmth that rubbed life back into her half-frozen legs and arms; and then her jaw dropped. Right next to her stood the most beautiful tree she had ever seen in her entire life.

At first her heart sang, but her momentary joy was crushed by the weight of an unimaginable sadness. 'How many people are you guiding home?' she asked the tree. 'All these lights. So many people lost.'

Touching her lips gently, Eulalie approached the enchanted tree. It burned with a thousand lights and yet not a single candle was in sight. Eulalie's eyes searched the ceiling above this magic tree for any signs of candle smoke but found none.

Every branch, every little twig and all available space was burdened with a treasure that might as well have tumbled out of the pages of her fairy-tale books.

Ruby, sapphire, emerald, amethyst and amber were frozen in permanent bubbles that swayed gently where they hung, suspended amid the branches– and when they touched, they sang with the crystalline voices of bluebells and cowslips. Their perfect bodies reflected the ever-changing lights and sent shadows and colours waltzing around the room. Eulalie tapped one strange green bubble. It bobbed and swayed. She leaned into the orb and giggled at how her nostrils grew large, her eyes bulged and lips puffed up in the reflection.

By some unknown spell, the lights on the tree changed from a slow dim then brightened to a flashing, *It must be a lightning tree.* Eulalie stifled a surprised gasp and watched the light lick the back of her hand and then she looked around the room. The light peppered everything around her in its firefly-like colours, outlining a ballad of brittle silhouettes on the canvas of this peculiar room.

Eulalie tiptoed around the tree so she wouldn't disturb the delicate web of wonder, forcing her gaze from one marvel to the next; crystal girls dancing on tiptoes, a comfortably padded man being pulled by a herd of deer, well-fed robins, stags with big noses, stars and a large heap of beautifully wrapped gifts.

'I also want to leave something here,' she exhaled in wonder. Excited, she skipped back to the fireplace and returned to the tree, dragging her bag behind her. Shoving both hands inside, she fumbled around and pulled out a couple of presents. One was wrapped in autumn leaves, the other in layers of spider web. They weren't as colourful as those under the tree, but they looked pretty special where she put them, nicely snuggled between other gifts on the thick carpet.

The carpet drew Eulalie's attention. 'It's so soft,' she said and wriggled her toes into the mossiness. 'I could sleep on this,' she marvelled.

'Blessed moonbeams.' Eulalie's heart skipped a beat. 'Look at the mess I've made. Footprints everywhere,' she whispered. She followed them back to the fireplace, each print appearing more sinful in the perfect room than the previous. 'Oh no, oh no, oh no,' Eulalie muttered and put her hand to her forehead. 'What have I done?' Hand marks, foot and boot stains and even a bum print was marking the place where she had first sidled out of the hearth. 'What am I going to do? I can't leave it like th...' Two of the friendliest, cosiest and largest socks she had ever seen hung on the wall on either side of the fireplace. Their welcome sight shocked her attention away from the disaster on the carpet.

Eulalie reached for the fabric, but then snatched her hand back. Squinting, she inspected her fingers and rubbed them on her thighs to clean off at least a token amount of dirt. Satisfied, she gently traced the fluffy outline of one sock. Someone had very cleverly appliqued a plump looking badger onto the knitwork. The other donned a red fox staring up at a peculiar white moon – it looked like Kahenna but was as white as ice. Maybe whoever made the sock ran out of red colouring.

Smiling, Eulalie lifted the sock off a little hook and lay it next to her bare foot. 'Giants. I'm in a house of giants,' she said and inspected the ceiling; it wasn't particularly high, but the sock was massive. She put both feet next to it – one bare and one booted and there still would have been space for a third foot. How wonderful would it feel to snuggle her frozen toes into such a fluffy miracle of tailoring? 'This would go right up to my knees,' she whispered and climbed out of the other boot.

Having completely forgotten about her dirty foot, Eulalie stretched the sock open, and was about to slip inside...

'I know where to find glue to fix this,' an unexpected voice said just behind her, shyly squeezing between the silence and the flickering lights.

THIRTY
DO TEARS HAVE FOOTPRINTS?

Eulalie swung around, one foot trapped the sock, the other stuck in its cloudy lip. A hiss escaped her mouth as she was hurled off balance and ended up neatly between two gifts, the bottom branches of the tree cradling her by the armpits. To add insult to injury, a crimson ball decoration swayed above her head, knocking her hat with every wave as if it was enjoying the spectacle and applauding for an encore.

Grunting, she untangled herself from the tree's flashing grip and stumbled up, ready for bruises, or whatever the mini giant child had in store for her.

'I…I'm sorry. I didn't mean to frighten you,' the child said. Her voice was laced with concern.

'Wha…uhm…oh.' Eulalie's words bounced like a split bag of marbles. Either the giant's daughter was very small, or she wasn't a giant after all, Eulalie realised when she faced up to the girl. She tried to dust off her embarrassment, hoping that there was a little bit of pride left beneath.

Sireneya's astonished gaze moved up and down Eulalie. Now that she was standing closer, the strange intruder looked even more like the Father Christmas she knew – all she had to do was stretch her imagination a little. This girl wore a red hat and collared tunic that even covered her neck – very useful on cold nights like tonight. Between the scrapes and dirt, her skin was stained in patches of white. Maybe if you looked quickly, those white stains could be confused with white hair and beard. And, she had come down the chimney bearing gifts.

Sireneya's heart beat in an excited drum ensemble; nervous, scared, confused, delighted; she didn't know what to say. There were all these Christmas adverts and films about Father

Christmas sneaking around houses, but they weren't too clear about what to do if you caught him red-handed in your house. 'I…I just thought we could fix this with glue. Are you…uhm…Father Christmas?' Sireneya asked. She climbed the stairs of her mind, searching cupboards and shelves for perhaps another meaning for the word *Father* that could fit better on a girl. She couldn't even find a rhyming word for it that fit. 'Are you his daughter? Are you from the cold north? Lapland?'

'What? I mean pardon? Glew?' Eulalie's words were stumbling; she just couldn't pull the correct sentences out of the string of confusion in which she felt entangled.

The child who was holding Rudolf was a little shorter than herself and wore a fluffy loose hanging suit with something that looked like a unicorn head dangling behind her for a hood. It almost looked as if she was wearing a *whole* unicorn skin. Her eyes were darker than the night – and were framed by the puffiness that comes with crying. Her long hair was tied back in a high, very untidy ponytail. In the dancing lights of the magic tree, Eulalie couldn't make out if it was brown or black. Her face was friendly and open but looks could be deceiving.

'Hello,' Eulalie said. Maybe she should start with the basics – individual words and hopefully proper sentences would follow.

'Hello. I'm Sireneya,' the girl said in a sunrise voice.

'Hello Sireneya. I'm Eulalie…and my dadda's name isn't Christmas. His name's Esau and he's a brute. And I'm actually from the south, not the north. And who is Glew? How can he help Rudolf?' Eulalie realised she had given the stranger her real name; too late to change that, now.

'Rudolf?' Sireneya's face lit up like a sunflower. Her eyes

poured all over the gargoyle and then pinned Eulalie in so much joy and excitement, that she couldn't help but smile too. 'Rudolf,' the girl whispered, scooping up the gargoyle and snuggling him to her cheek. Her body rocked from side to side and she fluttered another delighted look at Eulalie.

Eulalie's momma always said that when *she* smiled the wind changed, but this child had light that shone out of her dimples, her eyes … everywhere.

'Eulalie. I like that name. When you say it, it sounds like waves sizzling over sand,' Sireneya said.

Eulalie's mouth dropped. 'That… that's what my momma used to say. How did you know? You don't find my name… strange?' she asked.

'No. Of course not. You're from the South Pole. Not the North. And…and…the sleigh you arrived in is pulled by flying dragons and not reindeer. And Rudolf is a baby dragon.' Sireneya spoke with an accent that Eulalie had never heard before, but her words sounded soft and rounded off; almost like a song. 'Christmas is more magical than I ever imagined,' Sireneya said.

'It's actually a skiff, not a sleigh,' Eulalie said, not unkindly. 'Spookasem and I built a sleigh once, but it broke through the ice and is lying at the bottom of a lake…kind of like I was supposed to be lying at the bottom of a canal.' Eulalie scratched her head and frowned as she thought through the strange events that had brought her here. Maybe the girl knew about magic. Perhaps she had looked at her through a hidden window; or magic SoulGlass mirror like one of the old legends. How else could she have known that *Hocus Pocus* was a dragon in disguise? 'Anyway, who is Glew?' Eulalie asked.

'Glue is not a person. It's a thing. Don't you ever use glue when you fix toys? Almost anything can be fixed with glue. My brother even fixed my glasses once. His name is Reyn. He has a crush on a girl, you know? I know who it is, but I promised him I wouldn't tell.'

Eulalie had absolutely no idea what the little girl was talking about, but she was relieved that Glew wasn't a person.

'Come on then. Let's do it. We just have to be quiet,' Sireneya said. She turned and skipped to the stairs. 'It's up in my room.'

'Wait. Bring Rudolf back...'

Sireneya walked back to Eulalie and stopped inches from her. Still cradling Rudolf, she took Eulalie's cursed hand in hers, inspected it and then rubbed the dried blood and grime from the fingers. After a glance at Eulalie's dirty feet, her dark eyes searched her mapped face. Sireneya licked her thumb and rubbed at a scrape on her cheek and something on her chin.

She tutted. 'This won't do. Once we've fixed Rudolf, I'll grab my flannel and get you all cleaned up. You can't go and deliver presents when you're hiding behind so much dirt. If I was as pretty as you I'd show my face to the whole world,' she said. Her voice glittered like the sparkles from which rainbows grew. 'You've got freckles just like my mum.'

Eulalie was stumped. It had only been her momma that had ever called her pretty before. And now it happened twice on the same night. Eulalie wasn't used to the word *pretty*. It made her head spin – like eating too much sugar.

'Siren...wait,' Eulalie said and stopped the child as she turned to go up the steps. 'Why...why were you crying? Your eyes… I know what footprints crying leaves behind.'

Sireneya squinted but couldn't suppress another summery smile. 'So, Father Christmas *does* see everything,' she said as if talking to herself. 'My dad said you weren't real. But it's all ok now. I always knew you were. Come. Once we get to my room, be careful *and* be as quiet as a mouse. We don't want to wake the monster under my bed,' Sireneya said.

Before Eulalie could protest, she was nearly lifted off her feet as the little girl darted for the stairs, dragging her along.

Even though she was being man-handled into what sounded like the room of nightmares, Eulalie didn't mind. No-one apart from her mother and Spookasem had ever dared hold her hand without the fear of being cursed - and it felt kind of nice.

'Use the stepping stones. You'll be safe once you're on my bed,' Sireneya said. Her eyes were as serious as her words. 'And don't worry. It's all quiet at the moment,' Sireneya said. She edged the door open – just wide enough for a body to squeeze through.

Without any further delay, Sireneya disappeared into the room. Eulalie was very impressed. Sireneya's courage reminded her of fairy-tale bravery; small enough to fit on a page but large enough to rescue princes and princesses.

Eulalie peered through the gap made by the door, just to prepare herself for whatever she was letting herself into. She gasped and leaned against the wall for support. It wasn't the room of nightmares *at all*, but a room of wonder that she wouldn't even have been able to imagine if she tried for a hundred years.

THIRTY-ONE
MONSTERS EVERYWHERE

Yes, there *were* monsters in Sireneya's room – and fairies and mermenin and griffins and dragons probably too. But they were lurking in the pages of more books than Eulalie had freckles. Pictures coated the walls between the bookshelves showing children fighting real-life battles with wands or flying on broomsticks. Eulalie peeked again, just to make sure that she wasn't imagining it.

A corner table was so overburdened by towers of books, that its legs wilted and joints seemed in grave danger of collapsing under the weight of knowledge and stories. Shelves on two walls bloomed from the floor to the ceiling, hazy in the lines of brilliance that a little lamp at her bedside managed to cut through the dusty gloom.

The small room looked tiny from the outside, but was ready to burst with more worlds than there were stars. Eulalie shuffled over the threshold. Word-ghosts scuttled to their pages, hoping to be given the chance to tell their tales. The air was blessed with the perfume of parchment and knowledge. Sound and smell imploded as if she had been absorbed by the cotton of all the pages.

'… stepping stones…monster…'

Eulalie thought she had heard a voice trying to battle across the lagoon of fables, but she couldn't quite hone in on its source.

'Use the stepping stones. Quick,' Sireneya said. This time Eulalie found the voice; Sireneya was kneeling on her bed, her face seasoned in terror. 'Quick. The monster might get you.' She reached desperate fingers for Eulalie to grasp.

Eulalie couldn't see the monster that Sireneya was trying to avoid. The girl looked so serious, though, that she hopped onto the first stepping stone – cleverly disguised as a pair of pants. Then, with the practised agility of a cat, she skipped from shirt, to stripy sock, to dotted sock, to vest, to cap and landed safely on the bed.

'You made it. Wow, you're good,' Sireneya said. She threw her arms around Eulalie's neck and hugged her tight. Rudolf was lying quite comfortably on what looked like the softest pillow in the world.

'Ok, let's help Rudolf,' Sireneya said and slipped to the side of the bed. The girl lifted something from an open drawer and a heartbeat later, she was settled on her knees in front of Rudolf.

Eulalie joined her. She was terrified of blinking, just in case she missed one of the many marvels this room displayed. 'Where...are we?' Eulalie asked, trying not to sound too stupid. Everything just appeared too strange – too different. Even the window was hiding secrets behind a veil of snowflakes.

Eulalie turned to Sireneya, but the girl's attention was on the injured gargoyle.

'Could you hold this for me, please?' Sireneya asked. She gently took Eulalie's hand and guided it to hold Rudolf's wing against his little body. Leaning forwards, the child squeezed a tube against the broken edges smearing them with a strong-smelling liquid. 'Now press it. That's it. Just like that. It sets quickly,' she said. Keeping her eye on the wing, Sireneya twisted the cap back onto the tube of glue and then her eyes locked on the little glass playing cards that hung around Eulalie's neck.

Her careful hand cupped the glass and she looked at the little pictures. 'I have never seen anything so beautiful,' Sireneya whispered.

Eulalie followed her eyes and saw that she was staring at the puppeteer on the stilts, blowing a dandelion into the wind.

Sireneya smiled at some thought that obviously brought her joy and then she let go of the cards. 'Sorry,' Sireneya said. She had just remembered that Eulalie had asked her a question. 'We're in Wickhambreaux. Close to Canterbury.'

Eulalie was about to reply, when her attention was drawn back to the gargoyle. To her surprise, she could feel the wing tightening again. Baffled, she turned to Sireneya. 'I think... I think it's working. This Glew is ... like... magic,' she said.

'Yes,' Sireneya answered. 'The glue works very well. My dad doesn't want me to use it by myself, but he's always busy, so most things that I've asked him to fix never gets done. So, it's better if I do it myself.'

Eulalie marvelled at the little tube of glue and then slowly her fingers let go of the wing. 'I've never heard of Wickha...Wickham...it before,' she said softly.

'Not many people have. It's very pretty, though. It has many thatched-roof cottages, a little school and even a water-mill. I think it's a magic mill. I believe all mills are,' Sireneya said. 'I like this house. It's quiet here. My dad works from home now, but he used to go into London every day. He still has an office in Ravenscourt Park, but at least he doesn't have to go there too often. I'm glad *you* found it though. Being *Father* ... uhm ...Christmas girl, I'm sure you have a map of the *whole* world.'

Eulalie nearly tumbled off the bed. She managed to stop herself for the sake of Rudolf's delicate operation, otherwise she most probably would have. What had *happened* to her when her boat sank? Had she somehow managed to end up on the other side of the Tempest Barrier? She looked out of the window again. Snowflakes were clambering over each other to get into the room. *Ravenscourt Park?* If what Leroy had told her was true, then she must be floating in the air on a hovering mountain – on a *Skisle*.

A dull warmth in her pocket brought her back into the room – the peculiar heat felt like a pebble that had been baking in the sun. She fumbled inside and found Wynter's shell. It was giving off a strange heat.

Sireneya tapped the gargoyle's wing. 'It should be fine now.' She gently took Rudolf out of Eulalie's grasp. Her face beamed as she balanced the gargoyle on her palm in front of Eulalie.

This strange world she had tumbled into...or sank into...was filled with such wonder. How was that possible? 'It's... it's... all healed. Just a little scar,' Eulalie said and smiled. A particularly excited gust of wind shook the window.

'What is it like to live here, on ...' Eulalie tried to ask, but her words were suddenly cut short. Right in front of their eyes, the dull grey of the gargoyle turned to its original black. Its plump little stomach dropped right between his toes and he coughed for a breath, then stretched his injured wing and leg at the same time. The little creature turned his head and stared straight at Sireneya.

The astonished girl covered her mouth with her free hand. The gargoyle gifted her with a little sneeze and a shake-of-the-head. Then with a hop, he lifted off her hand, flapping his bat-like wings.

Sireneya shrieked in shock and awe. Eulalie's jaw dropped. Rudolf fluttered around the room twice, then landed on the floor and disappeared under the bed.

'Oh no, oh no, oh no, the monster will get him. The monster will devour Rudolf,' Sireneya cried.

Eulalie dived off the side of the bed and she, too, disappeared into the waiting arms of the shadows beneath.

'Sireneya. It's ok. Look, we're both fine. I've just been under your bed and survived. There's nothing under there,' Eulalie said when she reappeared with Rudolf moments later.

Rudolf hopped out of her cupped hands and landed on the bed. A cat-like purr vibrated at the back of his throat as he snuggled into Sireneya's knees. Sireneya's hands covered her face. Craning his neck, Rudolf tried to peer between her fingers. Uncertain how to console the terrified child, Eulalie put her hand on her shoulder and tapped her gently.

Once again, the shell in Eulalie's pocket heated up and she quickly transferred it to the other one. It had become so hot that it almost felt as if her leg was going to blister where it had pressed against her.

'There really isn't a monster there. I promise. I've just been there,' Eulalie said again.

'What if... what if its hiding in the shadows? Monsters like the dark,' Sireneya asked through a stream of tears.

Eulalie thought for a moment. Rudolf's ears twisted and he looked at Eulalie as if he, too, was expecting an answer. She then thought of the crimson night with all the sleeping monsters and of Leroy and the Marauders.

THIRTY-TWO
WE NEED THE DARK

'We *need* the dark. Stars don't shine without the dark. Bushbabies and owls live in the dark and they're cuddly,' Eulalie said.

Sireneya looked at her, her tongue working with that revelation.

'Sometimes...sometimes monsters aren't what we expect them to be...' Eulalie said.

Sireneya put her hand on little Rudolf. He liked that and snuggled into her. The room grew a bit brighter. Her lips must be promising a smile.

'I think... I think the monster under your bed is only visible to your heart. I don't think your eyes can see it. I also know such monsters.' Eulalie didn't really know what she wanted to say. While her mind was searching for words, she allowed her heart to do the talking. 'Those heart-monsters are difficult to defeat and most of the time other people can't see them.'

Sireneya eyed her with those large, dark eyes of hers, now framed by diamond droplets of tears. 'What ... what are your monsters?' she asked. She rubbed her nose with her sleeve.

Eulalie lifted her eyes to the ceiling beams as if searching for the courage to face *her* monster. 'My monster's not green, or slimy with long fangs or anything like that,' she said. 'It's just a silly voice. A voice that tells me that I'll never see my momma again.'

'Is she...how'd she...?' Sireneya struggled to find words that wouldn't sting.

'I don't know. My dadda was always shouting at her. Then one morning, after he had shouted at her all night, she was just gone. The next night my monster appeared.' The layer of bravery that blanketed her words was thin and fragile and cracked around the edges, making her voice quiver. She bit her lip, but then forced a smile.

'So, how do you chase the monster away?' Sireneya asked.

'How do I chase my monsters away? Mmm…' Eulalie squinted at the question. Then an answer-light flickered in her eyes. 'I smile. It's not always easy. Sometimes I cry, sometimes I shout and I know a few bad words too – so I say them sometimes. Smiling, I found is the best for me, though. My smile doesn't mean that I'm happy, but it shows the monsters that I'm strong. I don't think monsters like smiling very much. And monsters are afraid of those smile-weapons.' Eulalie captured Sireneya's gaze and held it tight. 'So, now that you know who my monster is, would you tell me yours?'

Sireneya tried to look away, but Eulalie's gaze was holding tight. She sighed and gave in. 'Kids at school. My monsters are some kids at school,' Sireneya whispered. 'They… they always try to find me to say nasty things. Even when I just want to sit and have my lunch, they'll come to me and say that I have no friends and … other stuff. There's five of them and one of me. I don't think that's fair. Now I hide. But hiding doesn't help, because I'm always scared. That fear always finds me. Especially when I'm lying in bed.' The little girl's voice was distant as if she was avoiding the dread she felt.

Eulalie shuddered as her anger sprang into life. 'Have…have you told anyone?' Eulalie managed to ask. There was an army of curses brewing on her tongue.

'No. My dad's always busy and I don't want to worry my mum. She's always on stage and needs to have a smile ready. If she worries about me, she might cry. And tears are heavier than smiles,' Sireneya said.

Rudolf purred.

'Look at my ear,' Eulalie finally said. She tipped her hat and pulled her hair out of the way, revealing a trail of scars leading to her no-ear. 'Everyone, apart from my momma thinks I'm cursed with all these white stains all over me. So, when I was little, someone tried to burn the stains away. It didn't work. Got my ear instead. My brother used to tease me so much about it that it felt as if his words were rocks that he was throwing at me. When my momma found out, she told me not to throw the rocks back, but to keep them. She said that my brother would run out of rocks at some stage or another and then I'll have enough to build a castle.'

Eulalie dropped her hair again. 'I'm not *exactly* sure what she meant. But I think I'm starting to understand. I don't know if it was my momma's words that had made me feel better, or just the fact that I had shared my fear with her. Anyway, something worked.'

Sireneya thought for a moment. 'Did your brother stop teasing you?' she asked.

'No, he still does,' Eulalie said and Sireneya's smile faded. 'But somehow his words don't feel like rocks anymore. And he can't throw them as hard anymore either. It's almost as if *he* hurts every time he throws one and I don't get angry. Maybe his rocks are bouncing back from the castle I've built and hitting *him*,' Eulalie said. She suddenly felt foolish. She didn't have a real answer for Sireneya and she didn't want to give her false hope. But then two shadows pooled in the dimples in the child's cheeks. Her smile was like moonrise, like the joy of the first star, like answers to all the world's most difficult questions. Eulalie's heart soared.

'I've got something for you,' Eulalie said. It was one of those moments where her heart spoke without consulting her mind first. She turned to the strange lantern that burnt without a flame and then looked at the walls. Eulalie didn't know why she did it; whatever her reasons, she never regretted it and whenever she thought about it afterwards, a feeling of comfortable warmth balled into the pit of her stomach. At that moment it just felt like the right thing to do.

Sireneya and Rudolf shifted closer.

Eulalie clasped the three glass playing cards that hung around her neck. She selected the glass card that Sireneya had admired earlier. Subconsciously she moved her pocket away from her thigh where the shell was once again burning her skin with a mysterious urgency.

'Farewell, my friend,' Eulalie whispered to the stilt-walker with the dandelion and lifted it over her head. She then spread the cord over the fabric of the lamp-shade, so that the little glass card came to a rest right in front of the glowing bubble. Then, while looking at the wall, she angled the lamp, until with a bit of clever manipulation, the light cast the perfect, enlarged silhouette of the puppeteer and the dandelion seeds on the wall. The dandelion seeds appeared to spread from wall to wall, carried by the imagination of the glassblower who had created it and the wind that was blowing while he had crafted the glass masterpiece.

It looked even prettier than when Eulalie and Spookasem had done the same in the mill using candles.

Sireneya and Rudolf stared at the walls and the floor in awe. Some of the dandelion seeds were cast on the carpet. Sireneya imagined them blowing under the bed and sweeping her monster away.

Before Eulalie could move, Sireneya had ensnared her in a tight embrace.

'Thank you,' Sireneya whispered.

'It's time for me to go,' Eulalie finally said. She had no idea how it was going to happen, but somehow the burning shell was urging her to return. Was that why Wynter had given it to her? Did he know that this was going to happen? All Eulalie knew, was that she had to get back to *Hocus Pocus*.

'Wait. I promised to help clean you up,' Sireneya said, before skipping to the washbasin in the corner of the room. With no monsters in sight anymore, she returned moments later wielding a wet cloth. 'To get to your boat, you'll have to climb onto the roof – and the only way up there from inside the house will be from my brother's room. His name is Reyn. He's annoying sometimes, but he's not bad really. And please don't tell him I told you, but he believes in mermaids. We'll try not to wake him, though.'

Sireneya pressed the wet flannel into Eulalie's smiling face; and not too gently.

Rudolf giggled, then fluttered around the room, pouncing expertly from dandelion seed to dandelion seed.

THIRTY-THREE

REYN

'Sireneya. What are you doing?' a boy asked, his voice sleep-muffled and a bit dream-confused.

Eulalie swung around to the bed. Even though Sireneya had assured her that her brother was a nice guy, she was still edgy. She knew all about older brothers and if she had ever been caught by her own brother sneaking around his room, it would end up as quite the bruise fest.

'Don't worry. I know that voice. He's still more asleep than awake,' Sireneya whispered, a little sprinkling of giggle spicing her voice.

Eulalie sniffed the air. This room didn't smell like a boy's room. She could smell *her* brother's room from anywhere on the second floor of *The Cross in the Roads*. That's most probably why she could hold her breath for so long – she would always try not to inhale the toxic fumes whenever she had an errand to run, a room to clean or a bed to make somewhere in that vicinity. 'This room is very tidy. Your boggarts must be very happy here,' Eulalie whispered.

Sireneya turned to her and frowned. She wasn't sure whether Eulalie was talking to her or not. Maybe there were boggarts in the South Pole where they made all the toys. Perhaps they were boggarts and not elves. She was about to ask Eulalie about it, but then her brother stirred and she stopped her question at her lips.

Eulalie winced as the shell in her pocket urged her on. She faced Sireneya. Rudolf was still sitting on her shoulder, and as if saying good bye, he snuggled into her neck and then hopped onto

Eulalie's head, almost pushing her hat over her eyes.

'Now remember to smile those monsters away,' she said to Sireneya and welcomed a hug.

'I will. Good luck with delivering all the presents,' Sireneya said.

'Siren? Who are you talking to?' the boy asked. This time he sounded surer of his words. The cocoon on the bed stirred and turned. Rudolf had such a fright that he fluttered off Eulalie's head and landed – not very elegantly at all, on the foot end of the bed.

'Rudolf. Come here,' Eulalie hissed.

'Go. Go. *Now* he's more awake than asleep,' Sireneya said and flung the window open. An explosion of snowflakes tumbled in, howling with joy as they were chased by the wind.

The boy on the bed sat up. 'Sirene, what on Earth are you doin…' he was stunned into silence as Rudolf landed on his feet with a flutter. Sitting on the ledge with one foot dangling in through the window and the other on the roof, Eulalie flung around to face him – and their eyes locked.

A shudder rushed through Eulalie in an explosion of heat. The boy's stare made her heart skip a beat; in fact, Eulalie grabbed for her chest, just in case her heart decided to leap out. Her fingers dared release her chest and she gripped the two remaining glass cards. Tearing her eyes from Reyn, she looked at the stained-glass image of the puppeteer with the mouse on his shoe and then back at the boy on the bed. It was the *same* person – they were even sitting the same way. Rudolf appeared to be quite content there on the boy's feet.

'Who…?' Reyn looked at Rudolf. 'What…?' The Gargoyle hopped onto his knee and then flapped back into the air, twice around the room and then out of the window.

Eulalie couldn't let go of Reyn's stare. In that instant she knew that she now had a new weapon to help fight her monsters – just a thought – just the memory of the beautiful boy sitting in the bed. Her puppeteer come to life. She urged her eyes to take in as much as she could, knowing that his imprint would be burnt into her memory forever, and then she rolled out of the window after the gargoyle.

Sireneya forced the window shut. A few straggling snowflakes hovered around her head. One landed on her nose and angling her lips, she blew at it.

'Sirene. Who… was that?' Reyn flung his duvet aside and rushed to the window. He tried to see out into the blizzard, but saw only his own, shocked expression reflected back at him. 'Sirene, who was that? What's going on? She could fall.' Not waiting for an answer, he flung the window open and pushed his head out into the maelstrom of flakes, wind and cold. There was no-one there, nothing; nothing he could see in the dark beyond the whirling white anyway. He battled the window closed, severing the howling gale that was blasting into his room. Snowflakes dropped by the abrupt disappearance of the wind, glittered down in the sudden velvet silence.

'Sireneya, who was that?' he asked, every line and shadow on his face emphasising his concern.

'Father Christmas. It was Father Christmas and Rudolf…' Something heavy scraped on the roof just above their heads and then fell silent again. 'You see; I told you he was real. And *he* is *actually* a she,' Sireneya said.

With a smile kindled by innocence and burning with the fires of smugness, Sireneya skipped out of her brother's bedroom.

*

Sireneya's night-light turned slowly. Normally, as it performed its programmed rotation, it would listen to the irregular breathing of a child who was terrified of monsters, but tonight it hardly heard any breathing at all.

Worried, it slowed down and cast its hearing deeper into the room – yes, there it was. A tender cotton of breathing filled the spaces where silence normally dwelled. It was the same child, yes, but her breathing was different. Her every breath hummed peacefully in time with the dandelion seeds that floated across the walls and drifted over a carpet where stepping stones were no longer necessary. The longer you looked, the more the seeds didn't look like seeds at all, but like forests and towers and castles and cottages and little isles floating like an enchanted world in the clouds.

Tap-creak, shuffle. Tap-creak, shuffle. Tap-creak. Weighed down by lack of sleep and half-blinded by dream confusion, Sireneya's dad made his way down the stairs and stopped. Finger marks stretched along the wall next to him. Leaning over the bannister he looked down.

'Footprints. Burglars,' he hissed and tried to turn, but he slipped and ended up at the bottom of the stairs with the promise of many bruises on his derriere.

Right between his feet lay a very large boot. His nose wriggled.

Careful not to get his own fingerprints over the evidence,

he pinched it between his thumb and forefinger and lifted it out of the way. He had never seen a boot like that in any shop before; unbranded and a round-nosed tip that yawned like Charlie Chaplin's used to.

His eyes then followed the pitter-patter of prints that danced from the hearth around the carpet. Afraid of what he might see, he squinted at the Christmas Tree. Nothing appeared to be stolen, but new gifts lay snuggled between the old; gifts that appeared to be wrapped in cobwebs and leaves.

THIRTY-FOUR
BUY SOME TIME

Spookasem kept glancing back at the scoop wheel and then the water, hoping that Eulalie would miraculously make her re-appearance. 'The wheel is slowing down,' he said. 'Why do I have a bad feeling about this?'

Cu-clunk, cu-clunk, cu, cu, cu...Whatever had driven the wheel had run out of energy. Out-of-breath it stopped and rocked backwards and forwards, coils, springs, dials and cogs tapping like a run-away heart.

'Aaargh, merciful moonbeams,' Spookasem shouted. He rushed to the wheel and gripped one of the slimy spokes. Gritting his teeth, he pushed it as hard as he could. The wheel teased him with a measly sway. 'Coome ooon.' He changed position and this time turned and leaned back, pulling so hard that his heels sliced two paths in the unseen algae under the water.

Waves of panic blistered his insides. 'Stupid wheel.' He lashed out at the wooden monstrosity aiming a kick at it.

'Ooouch.' The Inkling knotted his fingers round his shin and hopped deeper into the water. 'Eulalie, I think it's time for you to ret...' A huge bulge of water lifted up in front of him. It looked as if a monster had blown an enormous bubble that was about to pop. The mountainous surge rolled into him. Just before the water engulfed him completely, he thought he saw the word *Toktokki* emerging strangely distorted through the bubbling water.

Spookasem was rolled, tumbled and finally spat out onto the stony shore of the canal. Spluttering and coughing, the Inkling righted himself and sat up. Through his ruined fringe – that now covered his eyes like a wedding veil - he saw Eulalie's boat lift out of the water and sink down again. This time there was a deep *clunk* when it hit the bottom of the canal.

'Eulalie.' Spookasem dived towards the boat, just as Eulalie came up from beneath and his head hit her straight in the stomach. Doubling over, she fell on top of him, pushing him under the water.

'Spook,' she squeezed out with the last of her breath. Together, the two bedraggled souls pulled each other out of the water.

'Spook, I think you've broken my ribs,' she groaned, but the rest of her words disappeared when the Inkling flung his arms around her neck.

'I thought you had drowned. I thought you were dead.' The Inkling spluttered and sobbed without an inkling of shame.

'It's ok. I'm alive. Don't worry. I'm alive,' Eulalie said, trying to console her best friend.

Through waterfalls of relief, Spookasem could make out Rudolf, who was perched on the prow of Eulalie's battered little boat which was almost completely submerged. The gargoyle looked quite majestic like a proper figure-head until he yawned and snuggled himself into a puffy little ball.

*

'I swear we're going in circles. We've walked past that Man-Grove tree three times now and we're not getting any closer to *The Cross in the Roads*,' Spookasem said, sounding quite exasperated.

Eulalie stopped and felt her pockets. Wynter's shell was still there, but it didn't burn anymore. 'I wish we still had the cord,' she said. 'Anyway, don't worry. We'll get th...'

Her words were rudely interrupted by an all too familiar

voice dressed in icicles.

'Not so fast. We have some unfinished business,' it called out.

Eulalie's heart sank. She flung around. Two masked figures were running towards her. The voice was definitely Leroy's. She didn't recognise his companion.

'Run!' Barefoot, Eulalie sped off towards the tavern, but knew that it was futile and that she would most probably end up exactly at the same place again. 'Stop playing your tricks,' she hissed at Kahenna. The enormous waning crimson moon hung low and heavy in the night sky. She seemed droopy-eyed after such a long, adventurous night.

'I thought you needed her alive,' Leroy said loud enough for Eulalie to hear.

'Shut up, imbecile.' That was *M* again. *M* was back.

Moments later an ear-shattering explosion shattered the night and sliced a path through the dark. Little sparks of flame scuttered past Eulalie and something fractured one of the Mangrove trees just to her right. Flying splinters, mud and bits of wood cut into her arm and face. She screamed and fell over, covering her eyes.

'Get up, get up.' Spookasem gripped her under her arm and forced her back onto her feet. 'He's gonna use that weapon again.' Spook was looking back and moments later a second explosion thundered past them. This one landed in a pool of muddy water, sending sharp lines of water splashing into them.

'Down. Down. He's aiming…' The Inkling's voice was interrupted by the ominous *click* that had also preceded the other two explosions. Eulalie covered her head with her hands and rolled into a muddy pond as a rush of air, fire and noise brushed over her head.

'Spook, my ears. I can't hear anything.' Eulalie rolled over and stumbled up. A high-pitched white-hot noise rang in her ears.

She looked back to see the two Marauders being hassled by a huge gargoyle.

'Get away. Get away, Demon,' Leroy shouted, shaking his weapon at another dive from the large gargoyle.

'Look. It's Rudolf's momma; she's come to save us,' Eulalie cheered in momentary joy.

The large gargoyle roared as she swooped down onto the hunters and they, too, dived for cover. One of the Marauders lifted one of those thunder sticks and less than a heartbeat later, it burst lines of fire and thick white smoke. Rudolf's mum veered and fell.

'She's been hit,' Spookasem gasped and grabbed Rudolf, just as the little gargoyle lifted off. He squealed and struggled in the Inkling's hands.

'She's...she's fine. Spook look.' Rudolf's momma stretched her wings inches from the swamp and swooped into the air again.

'She's distracting them. Run.' Eulalie was about to head off back to the tavern – even though they had been trying that for what had felt like far too many turns of the hourglass – when a little white moth flittered up from the undergrowth in front of her. Eulalie could have sworn that the moth looked like a tiny person with very fluffy wings as it floated past her in its drunken dance.

'Eulalie. Come on.' Spookasem was already paces ahead of her.

'No. This way. Follow the fair...the moth,' she said.

The Inkling turned. 'Eulalie. You are running *away* from

the tavern. Blessed moons. Follow the moth. Aaargh.' The Inkling ground his teeth, rolled his eyes and followed Eulalie into a nearby copse of trees. 'We definitely didn't come this way earlier,' he groaned.

'I've kind of lost the moth,' Eulalie said when Spookasem and Rudolf had caught up to her. She was standing ankle deep in a small, shy lake that was cowering between the trees.

'Maybe you didn't hear me earlier, but the tavern is the other way,' the Inkling said. Rudolf was sitting on his shoulder looking back. A low growl was humming from the back of the gargoyle's throat and all his hairs were standing on end. He almost looked like a porcupine with wings.

'I just had a feeling we had to follow it. We can't go back now. If we cross the lake here, we won't leave any footprints,' Eulalie said and stepped onto the first stepping stone. Knobbly, weed-like algae grew on the rock, dripped over its side and hung suspended in the dark water.

'Eulalie…' Spookasem tried.

'Come,' she urged.

'We could just as easily have gone around,' Spookasem muttered. With a sigh, he balanced on the first mucky stone and followed Eulalie.

*

If Eulalie, Spookasem and Rudolf had been *under* the water, they would not have seen the mere sand, stone, weeds and water they would have expected. The stepping stones they hopped, skipped and jumped over, were in fact *not* stones resting on the lake bed at all. Kahenna, the crimson moon saw things for what

225

they really were. Her ruby light seeped into the cold and wet and unveiled what usually went unseen. These moss and lichen-covered stones were in fact the tops of the heads of a swamp troll, a handful of water sprites, a sinister Shellycoat and an unruly Urisk.

The swamp troll had so much padding growing on his head, he didn't mind being tapped on, but the Shellycoat and the Urisk didn't like it at all. When Spookasem had made it across, the Shellycoat rubbed the bumps and newly formed bruises on his head and turned to the other water fey and said, 'the next animal to use my head to keep his feet dry, I'm going to capture, pull under the water and step on his head a few times. See how he likes it.'

'I'll help,' the Urisk replied. Even though his tough head wasn't really bruised, he was just up for some mischief.

Moments later, Leroy and *M* burst from the trees and stopped at the shore of the lake.

'Go after them. Use the stepping stones,' *M* barked at Leroy. 'I'll go around and cut them off in case they decide to go that way.'

*

'Eulalie. I don't know what happened to the Marauder who was just behind us. One moment he was there and the next, he had vanished; into thin air,' the Inkling said. He cupped his hand over his brow and peered deeper into the gloom. 'He wasn't *that* far behind.'

'The other one's still there. The dangerous one. The one they call *M*,' Eulalie said. She hunkered down next to the Inkling. 'There.' Eulalie moved Spookasem's chin to guide his head to the right place.

'Ah…oh…I think I see him,' the Inkling answered. 'I feel his eyes searching for us.'

'Yes. Me too,' Eulalie said. 'But the shadows aren't kind to him.' Still crouched down, she looked around. 'The old church is just beyond this rise. We could try and hide there.' She pointed at a very overgrown incline.

'I don't think that the ruins are such a good idea. There's not much that remains of it. Just some bricks and one window. Even that's most probably toppled down by now,' Spookasem said.

'We've got to try. He's going to catch up to us soon. I don't …'

'Freckles. What's that?' Spookasem interrupted her.

Eulalie nearly jumped out of her skin when the Inkling's hand slammed down onto her wrist.

'You scared the life out of me…' she gasped. She followed his gaze, though. A little light appeared to flicker in the entanglement of trees behind the Marauder. For a moment, Eulalie thought that it might have just been a reflection, but then another appeared.

'There's another…' Spookasem said.

'Shhh. Yes, I see,' Eulalie said. Then she focused her gaze to the tops of the trees. Yes. Must be. It was too far to be certain, but Eulalie thought she knew exactly what was happening.

'Follow my finger, Spookasem. Do you see that bushy bit in that tree? It might just look like a deeper shadow but…'

'Mistletoe,' The Inkling said.

'Yes. You're right,' Eulalie said.

'So….?'

'On a Crimson Night, mistletoe is more than just sticky leaves. Come. Someone is buying us some time.' She quickly put her hand into her pocket and squeezed the little shell as if to say thank you to Wynter and the other mistletoe nest-builders.

Using the undergrowth for cover, they crept up the rise. If the ferns and brambles around them hadn't hissed in their passing, they might have heard naughty giggles chime in the distance.

Moments later they broke through the wall of undergrowth and stared at a vast expanse of the swamp. There was nothing to hide them. Eulalie's heart sank. 'There…there's just a wall and a window left. The church is gone,' Eulalie said. The few straggly dead trees, conducting their sinister symphony of mist and moonlight wouldn't be helpful either.

Spookasem didn't know what to say.

'We've got to try. That's all we have,' Eulalie said.

THIRTY-FIVE
THE GATEKEEPER

A brilliant kingfisher watched two bedraggled specimens approach. One appeared to have washed her hair in Kahenna's light and was clad in layers of secrets, while the other flowed like ink dropped into a pond of water.

The shimmering bird quickly wiped the fish scales from his beak, making sure his lips matched Kahenna's glow. Then he hopped onto a log next to the window and ruffled his feathers. His sapphire downs glimmered like a fortune-teller's voice.

'You've got to pay before I can let you through.' Where a blink of an eye earlier a kingfisher had been showing off his plumage, an old man now stood, leaning against the lone-standing wall. Not even Kahenna's vivid red light could dampen the brilliance of his iridescent grey hair that shone blue in the dark; not even the shadows cast by Kahenna's curious stare could hide the knowing, ever-curious glint in his eye.

Eulalie frowned at the wall that housed the window. 'We...we can just go around it,' she said.

Spookasem stole a step in that direction.

'You could, but that would be the easy option. And we all know that easy solutions sow the seeds to plants that have the potential to grow problematic roots later,' the man said and smacked his lips together as if he was still chewing on some fishy afterthought.

'The world through the window is a very different place to the world around the wall,' the old man said when Eulalie and the Inkling failed to respond. He flicked something into his mouth that crunched as he chewed. 'These two worlds might look similar, but looks, as you know, can be deceiving. It's the subtle differences that matter.'

Eulalie gasped and her face lit up. 'Are you the Gatekeeper?' she asked.

The old man stole a quick wink at the window and then looked back at Eulalie. 'Correct me if I'm wrong, but I don't see a gate anywhere. A window. No gate,' he said.

Eulalie looked back at the trees. The Marauder wouldn't be fooled for long. He'd be back on their trail soon enough. 'We're in quite a hurry,' she said. 'Are you the g…the Keeper or not?'

'M'name's Halcyon; I do a spot of fishing at times and I like perching close to the wall. I *keep* no gates, but I intend to keep a close *eye* on that window,' he said.

Halcyon lifted a brow and again popped something into his mouth. Either he was really enjoying whatever he was eating, or he was trying to draw Eulalie's attention to the snack.

'Eulalie. We've got to hurry. Let's go,' the Inkling said. He was losing patience.

'Wait. Spook. We've got to go through the window,' Eulalie said. 'I… think.'

She eyed Halcyon when she said that. She knew all about searching eyes. Words and shadows and lines on skin could lie, but it was near impossible for a lie to find any place to hide within the soul-vacuum of the eyes.

Halcyon put his hand into his pocket and was about to put whatever he had found into his mouth, when Eulalie stopped him.

'Wait, that was mine. I *have* paid,' she said.

Halcyon looked at the little carrot coin, turned it this way and that and then flicked it into his mouth.

'It's gone now.' He smiled. And *you* didn't give it to me, someone else did.'

'That's not fair,' Eulalie said. She looked back. The undergrowth shook. 'It was me who gave it to him... to Wynter. And I don't think I've got any left.' She emptied the contents of her bag at the Gatekeeper's feet, searching not only for a carrot or parsnip coin she might have missed, but anything that she could use as their payment.

'You mentioned Wynter,' Halcyon said. 'I know that little fellow quite well. He doesn't easily show himself. A friend of Wynter's is a friend of mine. How do I know that you're telling the truth about him though?'

The wind howled a sudden gust as Eulalie smiled. *That* she could easily do. 'How about this?' She took Wynter's shell out of her pocket and held it out to him. Her stained palm spread wide like her joy as she showed him the shell on the palm of her hand.

'Ooh. Now that looks interesting.' He pinched it between thumb and forefinger and held it up to the moon. 'Very interesting,' he said.

'Eulalie. He's coming.' Spookasem's voice was spiced with chilli-hot worry.

'Please sir,' Eulalie begged.

'Yes. This will do. Off you go.' Halcyon reached over and opened the window for them.

'Spook. You go first.' Eulalie lunged her knee into place and cupped her hand for him to use as a stepping stone to make it through.

Spookasem opened his mouth to protest, but one quick glance back at the approaching Marauder had him convinced. 'Ok.' The Inkling's voice had risen a pitch or two. He hugged Rudolf to his chest and stepped onto Eulalie's hand. Moments later, she had him through, albeit head first.

Eulalie looked around. The Marauder had stopped and was aiming that stick at her. The white and the lights and the sparks came first. Moments later the noise roared red-hot out of the angry smoke. His aim was wild and part of the wall burst into dust and stone, showering Eulalie in an unequivocal rage. She screamed, covered her head and hopped up, her stomach landing on the window ledge.

Legs flailing, she wriggled through.

The moment she landed – half on shoulder and half on side of face, another explosion cracked the wall.

'Quick.' Spookasem dragged her by the scruff of her collar and they flattened themselves into the wall beneath the window.

'Oh no,' Spookasem cried. 'He's doing it again. Rudolf's turning to stone.'

'Rudolf, no,' Eulalie cried. Rudolf's body was already hardening. Not knowing what was happening, his large eye's blinked slowly. A little tear dropped down his cheek, turning to a glinting diamond on the way down.

'Watch out,' Eulalie said. A clawed hand reached through the window and swiped inches from their heads as they rolled out of the way. Rudolf squeaked. A heartbeat later a large gargoyle's face appeared at the window. The mother gargoyle stretched her arms through the window to reach for Rudolf. Her skin creaked and cracked, dark arms hardening into a dull grey.

'It's the mother,' Eulalie called. 'She wants Rudolf. But she's also turning to stone here.'

With a heart-wrenching cry, the mother gargoyle pulled her arms back before they completely turned to stone.

Without hesitation, Eulalie kissed the gargoyle on his spiky head. 'Spookasem. Help. I need...'

Before Eulalie could finish her sentence, the Inkling had dropped onto his hands and knees under the window. 'Don't make a habit of this. Now hurry,' he said.

Using him as a step, Eulalie lifted Rudolf up to the window. Rudolf's mum was crouched on the other side. Flexing the life back into her fingers, she was watching the Marauder take aim.

An explosion shattered the night air and the wall shook. The mother gargoyle fluttered out of the way but landed under the window again.

'Here. Quick,' Eulalie said while leaning Rudolf towards her. As soon as she had him through the window, the baby started softening up again. The hard bits around his cheeks cracked as his lips pulled into a smile. The mother gargoyle took the baby from Eulalie with impossible gentleness and then chained Eulalie with her stare.

Within that one, eternal moment, Eulalie stared into the soul of a monster – and it was beautiful. Over the gargoyle's shoulder, the man was pouring something down the tip of his weapon.

It's all about the heart, Eulalie thought. *It's our hearts that make us beautiful or make us monsters. That's why our hearts are kept in cages – rib cages. To see if someone is a monster, we have to look past the outside and to the inside.*

The wall vibrated as the mother gargoyle pushed away from it with her heavy claws, severing their soul-to-soul connection. Eulalie ducked, shielding her face from the gust of wind the gargoyles' wings left behind. Rudolf fluttered close behind her – his distracted grace reminding her of the flight of a butterfly. They were followed by the blue flash of a kingfisher.

The Marauder arrived two heartbeats later and stormed around the wall. Even though Eulalie and Spookasem stood there in full view, he couldn't see them.

He stepped back, frowned and peeked through the window. This time he saw the child he had been chasing…and a shadow that somehow didn't appear to belong to anything. He hoisted the blunderbuss' strap around his shoulders and pulled himself into the window but slipped and fell back. 'Aaargh,' he shouted and tried again. This time his hands slipped. 'What treachery is this?' Again, he tried. Again, he failed. This time he cursed.

Eulalie was clutching her heart, her eyes wide in disbelief. 'We've made it. He…he can't get through. He hasn't paid. He's still lost in the Crimson Night and we're not. We've made it,' she cried.

'Are you sure?' the Inkling asked, his eyes still locked on the Marauder's appearing and disappearing masked face as his relentless desperation to get through the window yielded nothing but violent cursing.

'Yes Spook. We're safe from him,' Eulalie said.

'Well, in that case,' Spookasem said and shoved his thumbs into his ears, waving his fingers at the Marauder. 'Nyaaaaaaaa,' he stuck out his tongue.

THIRTY-SIX

NEVER EMPTY-HANDED

'It's number seventeen. I've found number seventeenaaaaargh.' The old, weather-thinned shutters couldn't muffle Lazaro's squeals of terror.

Eulalie's hand clutched the shaft of the weathervane, the other pulled at a locked shutter. She flattened her nose and cheek into the gap, stealing a peek through one of the third-floor windows of the many-turreted tavern. She caught a momentary glimpse of what appeared to be the local feral goose chasing Lazaro down the corridor and disappearing around the corner.

'That wasn't *P17* – it was …a goose? I never let Mr Grumpyfeathers into the tavern. Well, I invited him, but he wouldn't come,' Eulalie said. Frowning, she turned to her Inkling, whose droopy eyes just managed to peek over his fingers where his palms pressed into his cheeks. Sitting on his haunches on an age-forgotten chimney, he was staring at the nothing that floated in front of his face. A long, wheezy sigh spoke of a distant melancholy.

'Spookasem…it was Mr Grumpyfeathers…the goose. And I think there was poop on his head…not the goose's, my brother's… why the long face?' Eulalie asked.

Another sigh followed. '*Hocus Pocus* is barnacle bait. We've come back empty handed. We hardly accomplished anything we set out to do. Our map is gone. And I miss Rudolf.' His words were weighed down by the after-adventure-blues.

Eulalie hopped up next to the Inkling. She nudged his hip with her derriere until he shifted to give her a bit more brick to sit on. Then, after putting her arm around his shoulder, she, too, found that dreamy nothing and stared.

Eulalie's other hand strayed to the glass cards that hung

around her neck. It was the missing third one that got her attention. Pinching her eyes shut, the swirling colours behind her eyes took shape in the form of a puppeteer standing stooped over Sireneya's bed. Softly he stilt-limped around the wooden frame, bent over to avoid the ceiling. A shaft of light strayed to his hand and face, throwing a dust-filled spotlight onto a silver dandelion head he gently cradled in his fingers.

The puppeteer, who now looked exactly like Reyn, leaned his lips to the seed. He blew on the dandelion so softly, that it rather looked as if he breathed a secret upon it. In a hiss as soft as early spring, the little secrets sprang free and pirouetted around the room. The girl in the bed didn't look like Sireneya anymore. One cheeky seed settled on the sleeping child's freckled nose. She raised a stained hand to tickle it out of the way.

Eulalie's smile tiptoed around her heart. 'Spookasem,' she said. 'We didn't come back empty handed. *Hocus Pocus* might get a few more barnacles, but all dragons need scales. Every new barnacle just makes her look more like what she is like when I close my eyes.' She looked at her toes. She wiggled them. 'And my boots? I'm glad I lost them. Anyone can leave boot-prints, but only *I* can leave *me*-prints. With my feet and toes I've left a bit of me behind. If my momma is out there, the me-prints will be like a secret letter I've left for her.'

Spookasem sat up. Eulalie's words appeared to have struck a chord.

'And empty handed?' she continued. 'Yes. But if our hands were full, we wouldn't have been able to hold Rudolf. And carry him and fix him or give him back to his momma. Our hands had to be empty to be able to do that.'

'And the map?' he asked, already feeling much better.

'Why hold onto a map that someone else made?' she asked. 'Isn't it better to make our own? Then we can include what *we've* seen with *our* eyes and *our* hearts and even include our dreams.'

Spookasem didn't have to ask. Eulalie felt his question when his shoulder stiffened.

'No,' she said and sighed. 'We didn't find my momma. But...' she swallowed at two tears. One got away. 'But we *did* things tonight that would make her proud. I did things that *she* would have done. And for the moment, that's good enough for me.'

The weathervane creaked and her hair lifted in the breeze. Despite her exhaustion, she was beaming. Despite her bruises, she was exhilarated. Despite her dadda and brother's voices that tried their best to bring the monsters back, she smiled broad and wide like a bright spring morning.

Eulalie stole a sneaky glance at Spookasem and she saw him smiling too. His elbow gently found her rib, and she shoulder-nudged him back.

Monsters scattered – for the moment at least.

'If you don't mind...' Spookasem's voice broke the enchantment. The Inkling reached down the front of his tunic and pulled out a thin, gnarled stick. 'If you'll be ok here, then maybe...'

Eulalie thought perhaps she knew what he wanted to go and do. She smiled as she thought of the pictures she had seen on Sireneya's bedroom wall. Thinking back now, she was certain that the heroic girl hadn't been alone in the pictures. Had Spookasem been there too? 'See you soon,' she said, licked the ink on the back of her hand and rubbed it.

'Not if I see you first.' Spookasem's voice frayed like his outline, wavered like the air above a flame and then disappeared.

With the help of the shadows and some roof tiles, Eulalie made it to her locked bedroom window. She didn't mind the fact that it was locked – it would take her only moments to get inside; she had managed to get past the Gatekeeper, after all.

Using the rusty old nail that she kept under a nearby roof-tile for moments like these, she tickled the lock. Three heartbeats later, the lock gave a metallic chuckle and Eulalie slid the window open. She peeked inside. There was a puffed-up chicken sitting on her pillow.

'Eulalie, you will stop hiding this instant. Get down here and get these cursed birds out of my tavern... hiding...I'll show her a hiding.' Her dadda's voice vibrated through shutters and walls.

Yip, she was back.

A very tiny person, covered in the downs of the in-between landed on the windowsill, just in time to see a pair of scraped, swollen, mucky and stained bare feet slip into the tavern. Little bells chimed as she giggled and yawned. Frowning, she turned to the horizon to see if she could find Kahenna. The moon had already fallen asleep and all that remained of her passing was the feint ruby glimmer of her footprints that blew up from the horizon like wisps of far-off dust. Disappointed, she rubbed her drooping eye-lids with her knuckles and yawned again.

'Hello little moth,' Eulalie said to it.

The moth jumped. It was a good thing her back was turned to the window. It was never a good idea to show yourself too clearly to the human folk. Though she had doubts that this one really was entirely human.

'I've got something for you,' Eulalie said. Reaching into her pocket, she pulled out two little bottles. Spookasem's ink she returned, but the other she uncorked and tipped a little drop of moon water into an acorn cup for the moth.

The chicken behind her *clucked*. Eulalie just couldn't force her gaze from the swamp, though. The bloody footprints of Kahenna's passing outlined her world in enchanted contours, shadows and lines that made everything look brittle, almost like a stained-glass window. Somewhere in the clumps of trees below her, she imagined she could see little lights quiver where she had left candles. But they might just as well have been will-o'-the-wisps settling into nests of mistletoe.

Somehow the threat of her dadda didn't seem so bad after all and chasing after marked chickens, a duck and a mysterious goose in the legendary tavern called *The Cross in the Roads* sounded like a very good ending to an adventure-filled evening. Out there, what felt like a lifetime had crept by; in the tavern, not even a full turn of the hourglass seemed to have passed.

Until Kahenna would return again, she and her best friend, Spookasem, would keep a close vigil on the town and village noticeboards for any important announcements about lost souls who needed guiding home from the red. Because she and Spookasem knew the way now – well, sort of, it was their responsibility to rescue folk from the bleeding light. And maybe, she'd find out why the Marauders were catching Kahenna's creatures. And maybe, just maybe… momma… no she wouldn't think about it; that might chase away good luck.

In a few days' time, it would be Angetenar, the unseen

moon's turn to grace the night sky. Known as the *Bride of Tides,* she would drag behind her a gown of ocean and marry the waters of the surrounding rivers. Her wedding ceremony would flood the swamp and once again the landscape would change. Who knew what adventures would be lurking under the water? Who knew what answers about SoulGlass and floating worlds could be laid bare?

Clutching Reyn to her heart, she sped off into the tavern to face the music – the orchestra of familiar smells, choirs of boisterous voices and ballads of brittle silhouettes cast by the dancing lights of candles.

*

'Oh, hello. Back already?' *Old Knee-Cap,* the tree asked.

Shadows shifted and someone stepped through the undergrowth. A freckled hand reached for a book-shaped gift wrapped in leaves and spider webs cradled in the tree's gnarled arms.

'That's strange,' a familiar, yet unfamiliar voice said. 'I follow a pair of very adventurous footprints and I stumble upon this.'

The tree blinked and the visitor allowed the last of the shadows to drop by her feet.

'Oh, pardon me,' *Old Knee-Cap* said. 'For a moment I thought that you were somebody else.'

THE END

Gideon Kerk was born and raised in Africa, where he spent his young life fluttering between game reserves. He began writing at an early age; being chased by elephants and swimming in crocodile infested rivers appeared a little less frightening when merged with imaginary adventures.

After studying English literature, his work as a specialist English and Circus Skills teacher took him and his stories to the peaks and valleys of the Swiss Alps and the vast forests and plains of East Africa. Finally setting down roots in England, he now lives in Surrey with his wife and young son.

Between creating pages of story books and teaching English, he is hoping to put together the country's first Unicycle Quidditch league.